THE COMPLETE CASES
OF MARIANO MERCADO, VOLUME 1

THE COMPLETE CASES OF

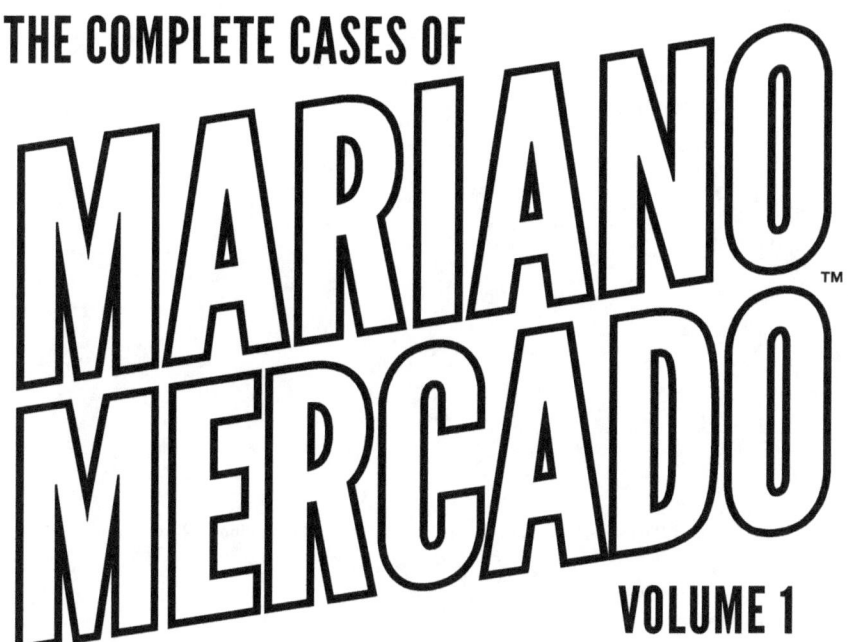

MARIANO MERCADO™

VOLUME 1

D.L. CHAMPION

ILLUSTRATIONS BY

JOHN FLEMING GOULD

BOSTON • 2016

TABLE OF CONTENTS

MEXICAN SLAYRIDE

BEAUTIFUL, SUNNY MEXICO, LAND OF TEQUILA AND TORTILLAS—AND MARIANO MERCADO, *DETECTIVE PARTICULAR*, THE SANGUINE *SEÑOR* WITH THE SANITARY PSYCHOSIS. EVEN MONEY WAS SLIGHTLY REPUGNANT TO MERCADO—THINK OF THE MILLIONS OF GERMS ON JUST ONE PESO NOTE!—BUT THIS WAS A MATTER OF HONOR. GENARO DIAZ, HIGH GOVERNMENT OFFICIAL, HAD BEEN BUTCHERED WITH AN AZTEC SACRIFICIAL KNIFE, AND THE LITTLE LATIN SHAMUS FOUND HIMSELF GIVING ENGLISH AND CRIMINOLOGY LESSONS TO A KILLER.

CHAPTER ONE
MICROBES AND MURDER

IT WAS an incredibly beautiful morning. The sun spangled the patio where I sat beneath the stretching branches of a huge Indian laurel. Far off in the distance, beyond the brick and plaster of Mexico City, towered the snow-capped twin peaks of Popocatepetl and Ixtaccihuatl, as majestic as they are unpronounceable.

On my right, hummingbirds, wings fluttering at magical speed, breakfasted off flaming bougainvillaea. On my left, hibiscus and poinsettia painted the stone wall of the house a bright crimson. The sky was as blue as the gaze of a Hollywood blonde, the grass as green as a thousand-dollar bill and equally satisfying.

If anyone had told me there was a corpse within thirty feet of me, I would have called for the wagon and two husky attendants to assist him into it.

I flicked the riding crop against the top of my highly polished boots and was possessed of such a sense of well-being that I didn't care how long Ruth Fuller kept me waiting. I inhaled deeply of the thin air and remained in a sort of static, comfortable coma.

I came out of it as I heard a heavy footfall and a harsh, grunting vocal sound. I looked up to see Harvey Fuller. His expression was neither cordial nor hospitable. He was a heavy man of something over fifty. He was dressed in a suit which had cost more money than my entire wardrobe. He was fat and the usual wrinkles on his full face were now enhanced by a dark frown upon his brow.

He came down from the veranda which formed the patio's perimeter, walked across the lawn and stood directly before me.

"Latham," he said, "you're an insensitive oaf. Hinting seems to have no effect on you. I shall, therefore, have to be more direct."

I stood up. "Don't bother," I told him. "I'll say it for you. Merely because I was once engaged to your daughter is no reason for me to call on her now that she is engaged to another man."

In the instant I was hurtling above the shoulder of the road, I remembered that when I had last read the speedometer, it had registered fifty.

"Precisely," he said. "Since you know that, why the devil are you here?"

"Ruth asked me to go riding with her. Since good Queen Victoria is dead, I see no reason why I should first obtain her father's permission."

He grunted. "You have no shame," he said. "She's an engaged girl and you should leave her alone. Besides, I can't stand draft dodgers."

That hurt. But I kept my temper.

"You know damned well I'm 4F. You know further that I'm recovering from a bad attack of pneumonia."

He shrugged beautifully padded shoulders. "Maybe," he said. "However, I consider anyone under thirty-eight a draft dodger."

"Do you?" I said. "And how old are you?"

"Fifty-one. Hell, you don't expect a man my age to be a soldier!"

"Of course not," I said. "Fifty-one, eh? That would have made you twenty-five in '18. What did you do in the last war, Fuller?"

THAT GOT him. Blood came up over the edge of his collar like lava. A botanist would have found the similarity of his color to the hibiscus most interesting. He knew quite well that I was aware of what he had done in the last war.

He had borrowed a couple of thousand dollars, built himself a munitions plant on credit and proceeded to roll up a fortune. Since that day he had kept on rolling it, right up to the umpteenth power. He was possessed of vastly more money than integrity, a fact which was probably also true when he only had the two grand. That, I reflected, was a rather bright thought and I said it aloud.

Fuller bit his lip, glared at me, then tacitly decided upon an armistice.

"Have you seen Diaz?" he asked.

"No. Is he supposed to be here?"

"He was due to meet me in the library here. I'm quite late."

"Ruth told me you were taking your first Spanish lesson this morning."

"I was going to, along with Walters. But Grew, who is going to teach us, called up and said he couldn't make it."

I lifted my eyebrows. "Walters?" I said. "I hardly think that boy needs any Spanish lessons."

"Why not?" he said sharply. "What the devil are you implying? You hate his guts because he's engaged to Ruth."

"All right," I said, "have it your way. Go along and see Diaz. I'll just keep waiting for Ruth."

He turned his head in the direction of the house and shouted: "José!"

A middle-aged Mexican shuffled out of the *sala*. José had come with the rented house. He was butler, *mozo, criado,* and general factotum. His principal talent was that he spoke English.

"Has Señor Diaz come?" asked Fuller.

The servant nodded. "He is in the library. He came forty minutes ago."

Fuller turned toward the house. On the veranda, he looked back at me.

"You'd better come along, too, Latham. Diaz can't speak English and I don't know a word of Spanish. Maybe we can use that broken-down dialect of yours."

"Your overwhelming courtesy in asking for favors," I said, "is irresistible."

I followed him into the house.

Evidently, the *dueño* who had leased the house furnished to Fuller was no bookworm. The library contained an old encyclopedia, two telephone books and a cheap Spanish dictionary. That was the only gesture it made to literature. For the rest it was comfortably furnished and its walls were criss-crossed with ancient Aztec weapons, knives, swords and mysteriously engraved machetes.

But beyond these furnishings, the room was empty. Fuller grunted. He took a cigar from a silver box on the desk. He did not offer me one.

"Now, where the devil is Diaz?" he growled.

I aimed my thumb in the direction of a lavatory which opened off the east wall. "Probably in there."

Fuller grunted again. He lit his cigar and we sat in a rather hostile silence for some ten minutes.

"For God's sake!" said Fuller. "What's he doing in the can all this time? Washing his socks? Latham, see if he's in there."

I got up and tried the lavatory door. It was not locked. I went inside. A moment later I thrust my head through the door jamb.

"He's here," I announced.

"Then tell him to come out."

"When he comes out," I said gravely, "someone will carry him."

Fuller cursed. "I never yet saw a Mexican who could carry his tequila. My God, has he passed out at this hour of the morning?"

"For eternity," I said.

FULLER STARED at me. His mouth gaped and his eyes opened. "You don't mean to say—"

"I do. He's dead. One of those Aztec sacrificial knives which was hanging on your wall is now reposing in his heart. Come and see."

Fuller stood up. He approached the lavatory cautiously, pushed his head into the washroom as if he feared someone were going to slug it with a baseball bat. Then he clapped a hand to his head, retreated to the library and sank, panting, into a heavily upholstered chair.

"This is a terrible thing, Latham," he said. "Terrible."

"What are you squawking about?" I asked him. "With Diaz out of the way you can get that concession on the Guerrero zinc mines with no difficulty at all. Hell, that's what you came down here for, isn't it?"

He didn't answer. He ran his fingers through his disappearing hair and groaned loudly.

A happy thought came to me.

"Maybe," I said, "you killed him."

He looked at me sorrowfully, an expression of pained sanctimony on his face. "Latham, he said earnestly, "how can you say such a thing?" He paused and looked thoughtful. "Wait a minute," he went on. "Maybe you killed him yourself. You were the only person here when I came in, except José."

"Fair enough," I said. "But I had no motive. Everyone in Mexico knows that Diaz, as the Government official in charge of such things, was opposed to granting you the concessions you wanted. On the other hand, his assistant, who succeeds to his office now, favored you. No, they can't pin it on me, Fuller. But they wouldn't have one hell of a lot of trouble pinning it on you."

His face no longer resembled the hibiscus. It was rather like the emerald green of the Indian laurels which I could see through the open door in the patio.

After a moment, he pulled himself together, got out of the chair and paced the floor.

"You're a fool," he said. "I couldn't have killed him. José saw me come in. You came in here with me. I had no opportunity to kill him. But I admit it looks bad. Bad for my reputation. Latham, we've got to look for the murderer."

"That should be worth something to you."

"It is. We'll notify the police. Then I'll engage a private detective. I'll give him ten thousand pesos."

"Why give it to a private dick?" I asked. "I'll tell you who killed Diaz for five thousand pesos."

He ceased his pacing and came to a West Point halt. "Who?"

"Walters," I said. "Jerry Walters, your prospective son-in-law."

"Latham," he said, "you're crazy. You hate that boy because Ruth's going to marry him. Why on earth should Walters kill Diaz?"

"Jealousy," I said. "Let's look the facts in the face. Ruth, even you must admit, is an unconscionable flirt. Walters is a hot tempered, possessive, jealous sort of a guy. During the past few weeks, Diaz and Ruth have been conducting a discreet flirtation. Nothing serious, of course, but enough to enrage Walters who resented it. Now, Walters is here when Diaz arrives. Walters quarrels with him, then snatches a knife from the wall and kills him. It's as simple as that."

"It's positively brilliant," he said. "Except for one minor fact that your malicious mind has overlooked. How the devil could Walters quarrel with Diaz when Walters doesn't speak one word of Spanish, and Diaz didn't know a syllable of English?"

"What makes you think Walters can't speak Spanish?"

"I *know* he can't. What makes you think he can?"

"I've heard him. But why waste time in this futile discussion? Call the coppers first. Then, if I prove beyond all doubt that Walters killed Diaz, will you give me five thousand pesos for the job?"

"Latham," he said, "you're a blockhead. It's not worth a nickel to me if you prove Walters is a murderer. It's not worth a nickel to me if you prove anything. I'm delighted that Diaz is dead. I don't give a damn if his murderer goes scot-free. But I've got to make myself look good. I've got to offer an authentic private detective a fat fee to try to find the killer. That'll sit well with the Government. Anything you do is worth nothing, even if you should be right, which would be extraordinary. "

I THOUGHT it out in great detail. I saw his viewpoint clearly enough. If the killer of Genaro Diaz was brought to book, well and good. If he wasn't, it didn't mean a great deal to Harvey Fuller. To anyone who knew him it was obvious Fuller was no murderer, even if his business ethics were not the same as those taught in Sunday school.

Moreover, as he had pointed out, my testimony and that of José would easily clear him from all suspicion. However, since he required favors from the Mexican Government, it would look good if, on the face of things, he spared no effort in attempting to track down Diaz' killer.

He needed the publicity which would follow his hiring a detective far more than he actually needed the criminal. On the other hand, there was my point of view. I was short of cash and a piece of ten thousand pesos would look very good. Besides, I don't like Jerry Walters at all and, most important, I had some evidence.

"Listen," I said, "suppose I told you that when I walked in here today, I heard voices coming from the library. I eavesdropped for a moment. I overheard Walters bawling out Diaz in Spanish, threatening to kill him if he didn't lay off Ruth."

"Really?" said Fuller skeptically. "And I suppose you heard Diaz' agonized cry as the knife went into his heart?"

"I did not. It was none of my business and I went along and sat in the patio where you found me. But what do you say to the rest of it?"

"I say, Latham, that I don't believe you. That no one else would, either. It can be easily proved that you don't like

Walters. It can be equally easily proved by scanning the records of the State Department that Walters has never before been out of the United States. It can further, doubtless, be proved that he never studied Spanish in college or anywhere else. All of which makes you look like a vicious and unmitigated liar."

"All right," I said restraining my temper. "I see what I'm up against. But will you call José and ask him at what time Walters came here this morning, what time he met Diaz in the library?"

Fuller nodded. "I'll do that because I'm certain that Walters wasn't here at all this morning. He told me he had some business at the embassy and would be tied up until lunch time."

"Call José."

CHAPTER TWO
MICROBE HUNTER

"**N**O, *SEÑOR*," said José a few moments later. "I have not seen the Señor Walters today. I was working in the garden when the Señor Latham came in. The gate was unlocked but I saw him enter. I did not see the Señor Walters at all."

"And when did you admit Señor Diaz?" asked Fuller.

"About a half hour ago."

"All right," said Fuller. "That's all."

José shuffled out of the room. Fuller regarded me triumphantly. "There you are," he said. "Even if Walters got in without José seeing him, how the devil did he get out again? There are two doors to the library. One opens on to the garden where José was working, the other to the patio where you sat. Since neither of you saw him, what is your conclusion, Latham? Perhaps you'll agree with me that you're a vicious liar."

I sighed. There was something very screwy going on here. I had never considered Jerry Walters any too bright, but it seemed to me that this time he had been far brighter than I.

"All right," I said. "For the time being, I'm a vicious liar. Now, may I offer you the use of my broken Spanish to call the police?"

"God," he said, "I'd forgotten that. Call them at once, Latham."

I called. In my limited Spanish I made it moderately clear that a Government official lay dead in Harvey Fuller's library. Their reaction was Latin, excited and voluble. After answering several questions I had hardly understood, I hung up.

"Good," said Fuller. "Now, Latham, go out and dig me up a private detective. I don't care how damned incompetent he is, either. I want the Government to know that I've wasted no time, that I have a man working on the case almost as soon as the coppers arrive."

I looked him squarely in the eyes. "You have an unmitigated gall," I told him. "You heap me with insults, then turn to me for favors."

"Favors?" said Harvey. "Look, you can speak this lingo more or less. It'll be easier for you to get a dick than for me. And it's hardly a favor. I'm offering ten thousand pesos. You can hold your man up for whatever commission you can get away with. From what I hear you can probably use a relatively honest dollar."

That was true enough. I could. Ten thousand pesos in Mexico is a great deal of money. I was sure I could chisel any private shamus down to a fraction of that fee.

"Well," said Fuller. "Do you know anyone?"

I scratched my head and recalled a weird evening of a week ago, in a honky-tonk *cantina*. I took a card from my wallet. It was immaculately white and expensively engraved. I handed it to Fuller. It read:

MARIANO MERCADO, DETECTIVE PARTICULAR
Investigaciones confidenciales Civiles y criminales

"O.K.," said Fuller. "As long as he's a professional, it's all right with me. Get him. Get him right away. It'll look better if it's known I have a man on the trail before the corpse is cold."

"All right," I said. "If he's in, I'll have him here within the hour. That'll just about give the coppers time to do their stuff and get out of the way."

"Get going." He glanced through the open doorway at the corpse, shook his head like a disapproving schoolmaster, and made a sad, clucking noise with his tongue. "Too bad," he said. "He was a young man, too."

"Don't drown yourself with those crocodile tears," I said over my shoulder. "His demise means a cold million bucks to you. Save the histrionics for the police department."

I could feel his glare on the back of my neck as I went out into the garden.

IT WAS almost at the gate when I ran into Ruth. She was a tall brunette with even features somewhat thrown out of symmetry by a spoiled, petulant mouth.

She gave me a smile which once had caused my heart to perform most unreasonable acrobatics. I noted with satisfaction that nothing of the sort happened now.

"Hi," she said. "Sorry I'm late. Had a lot of shopping to do. Hang on a minute. I can change in no time."

"I'm sorry, too," I said. "But we're not going riding now. You'd better go in and see your father. He needs you. I'll be back in a little while."

"Dad? Why, he's in the library with Diaz arguing about the concession, isn't he?"

"He's with Diaz," I said. "But he's not arguing. As I say, I'll see you later. I'm off to retain Mariano Mercado."

"Mariano Mercado? Who's he?"

I went out the gate without answering. One reason was that I wasn't sure of the answer anyway. I had met Mercado only once in my life and under odd circumstances. I hailed a cab, gave the driver the address and recalled the circumstances of my acquaintance with the *detective particular.*

On that day, exactly a week ago, I had been tired and depressed. True, my health was better than when I had left the States, but I was at loose ends spiritually and most certainly financially. Under the circumstances I decided to get mildly drunk. Since cash, or rather the lack of it, was one of my major concerns, I eschewed Ciro's, the Ritz and the other expensive saloons where the Americans gathered. I chose, instead, a tiny and none too reputable *cantina* hidden in an ill-lit byway in the eastern part of town.

I tossed my hat on the table, sat in the semi-seclusion of a paper-decorated booth and ordered a double rum. I sipped it and glanced dolefully around at my surroundings. The *cantina* consisted of a single long, narrow room. Opposite me the bar ran the length of the wall. In the rear a juke box vomited brass and woodwinds. A half a dozen *muchachas,* whose profession would have shocked and fascinated your Aunt Ida in Indianapolis, ambled about the room, essaying eagerly to detect the faintest glint of interest in any male customer's eye.

I was engaged upon my third double Bacardi when Mariano Mercado entered. Of course, at that time I did not know his name. All I knew was that I was gazing at a sartorial ensemble which would have caused a blind man to blink.

Mercado was a little man, short and springy. His complexion was the color of cafeteria coffee, his eyes black and shiny, his teeth as white as the snow-capped peak of Popocatepetl. He approached the bar rather mincingly in button-topped shoes and sat down.

I pushed my rum aside and studied his vestments. The suit with which he had caparisoned himself was a light and revolting green, his shirt was as yellow as a draft dodger, and his tie was a nice admixture of the hues of both suit and shirt. His shoes were the color of highly polished desert sand and his socks were silk and purple.

Now, I am no Thomas Craven when it comes to art and I am of the immovable opinion that Rembrandt and Maxfield Parrish are both excellent artists. Nevertheless, what little aestheticism there is in me rolled over and gagged as my eyes took in the picture of Mariano Mercado.

IGNORING MY rum, I watched him, fascinated. In a voice tinged with arrogance he ordered a bottle of *habanero* and a glass. When the bartender produced these articles, Mercado did not immediately pour his drink.

He lifted the glass to the light and examined it carefully. He took a tiny bottle from his pocket, uncorked it and dropped a globule of liquid from it into the glass. Then with the aid of a snowy white handkerchief, he swabbed the interior of the glass. He made a very thorough job of it, too.

After that he uncorked the *habanero* bottle, carefully wiped the place where the cork had been with his disinfected handkerchief, then poured himself a stiff drink. He drained it and then, setting the glass back on the bar, wiped his fingers off meticulously as if aware that as many germs could dwell on the outside of the beaker as in its interior.

I observed that neither the girls nor the bartender paid any attention to these odd drinking rites. I assumed, therefore, that he was a habitué of the place. I gathered up my rum again, but I kept my gaze on Mercado over the rim of my glass.

He knocked off three more *habaneros,* then he coughed. It was a slight, muffled cough, an ordinary common cough that could easily have emanated from as healthy a throat as that of Joe Louis. But from the expression on Mercado's face you would have thought it was the last gasp of a third-stage consumptive. His coffee-colored face became gray, his eyes opened wide and an expression of grave apprehension stamped itself on his features.

He slid from the bar stool where he sat and walked hastily over to the juke box, in the center of whose rococo exterior was a small mirror. Mercado bent down and stared at the reflection of his face. He opened his mouth, thrust out his tongue, examined its counterpart in the mirror like a Tiffany appraiser staring at a diamond, He pulled up his eyelids and scrutinized his pupils.

Then he straightened up again, reached into his coat pocket and produced another bottle. From this he extracted two pills which he popped into his mouth. He replaced this vial, groped again in his pocket and came up, this time, with a hard black object shaped like a fountain pen.

He unscrewed its top, whipped out a thermometer and stuck it in his mouth. Then he returned to the bar, sat quietly on the stool waiting for his temperature to register.

I emptied my glass and ordered it refilled. But I never took my attention from Mercado. He fascinated me. Apparently this was hypochondria run riot, a hundred and thirty-odd pounds of it wrapped up in a green suit which certainly would scare away any discriminating germ life.

At last he removed the thermometer from his mouth, read it, and made a clucking sound like an apprehensive old hen. He put the thermometer back in his pocket and turned back to the *habanero* like a man resolved on having a final fling ere Death knocks at his door on the morrow.

IT WAS then that the newsboy thrust his tousled black head through the swinging doors and cried out in accelerated Spanish. He spoke too rapidly for me to follow it entirely, but I heard the word *policía* spoken twice. I had lived in Mexico long enough to know what it meant.

It was a situation analogous to the New York coppers descending from time to time on dives and poolrooms for a check-up, a frisk, and to keep an eye on things generally. I was not surprised to find this happening to a *cantina* of this sort. I *was* rather surprised to note that the newsboy's announcement had, apparently, greatly interested Mariano Mercado.

He became suddenly alert. He glanced swiftly around the room. Then he slid off the stool again and headed for the juke box. In order to reach the instrument he had to pass my table. As he did so, his swinging green arm brushed against my hat and knocked it to the floor.

He paused and picked it up. He replaced it on the table top, flashed his white teeth at me and murmured, *"Mil perdones, señor,"* continued his march to the juke box and dropped a twenty-five centavo piece into its avid maw.

Thirty thousand decibels of *Pistol Packin' Mama* issued immediately from the loud speaker. Simultaneously three coppers came through the swinging doors. They looked professionally around the room. They saw Mercado standing by the music box, grinned and nudged each other.

Two of them lined up the more frowzy characters at the bar and searched them. One devoted his attention to Mercado. He patted Mercado's pockets hopefully and, I thought, seemed disappointed when he found nothing. Mercado, who had made no protest at the frisk, now brushed with his handkerchief those parts of his suit which the policeman's hand had touched.

The copper grinned unpleasantly at him, said something obscene to his companions and a moment later they were gone. Mercado looked after them, in reproach rather than anger. He shrugged his shoulders and sighed. He came over to my table.

"Con permiso, señor," he said. He lifted up my hat, revealing beneath it a huge .45 that looked like an aborted howitzer. He deftly dropped it in his coat pocket.

"Gracias, señor," he said.

As I stared at him, amazed, he whipped a card from his vest and handed it to me with a flourish.

"Sí necesita usted mi servicios..." he said, then turned on his heel and strode out into the night.

I blinked after him, then read the card which informed me that Mariano Mercado was a private detective who conducted confidential investigations, both civil and criminal.

I called the bartender over to clear up the item I failed to understand.

I said in my not too fluent Spanish: "The little man in the green suit. He is a detective?"

"*Sí, señor.*"

"Then why the hell does he find it necessary to plant his gun under my hat when the coppers come in?"

The bartender smiled. "But the Señor Mercado is not of the police, *señor*. He is the private detective. He is a clever one. He has outwitted the police on many occasions. For that they have withdrawn his pistol permit. That is why they search him every time they see him."

"So," I said, irritated, contemplating my night in the *cárcel* if the coppers had found me with an unlicensed gun, "he made me the fall guy, eh?"

What a fall guy was, the bartender, I knew, did not understand, but from his broad grin I knew also he was considering me the Mexican equivalent of one.

CHAPTER THREE

SEÑOR MERCADO — DETECTIVE PARTICULAR

THE OFFICE of Mariano Mercado, *detective particular*, was in the same apartment as his home. Both were on the third story of a weary building of plaster and stucco in the Calle de Madellin.

I dismissed my taxi and entered the house. The scurrying of a thousand rats punctuated my own footsteps as I mounted the protesting stairs. I knocked at the panels of the door which bore Mercado's card thumbtacked in its center. His familiar voice called out: *"Entre."*

The windows were covered with fine wire mesh and draped over them was a piece of heavy cheesecloth which effectively kept the sun out. The furniture was of plain wood. There was not a cushion, a pillow or a drape in sight.

At a severe desk in the middle of the room sat Mercado. On his left was a huge ledger. The remainder of the space was occupied by an array of bottles, none of them of any alcoholic content. Hanging at the side of his desk was a large oblong of ruled paper which looked vaguely familiar to me. I peered through the gloom of the room and examined it. It was a temperature chart, and none ever had as even an ink mark across it.

Mariano Mercado showed me his glittering white teeth. He waved me to a severe straight-backed chair. He said in Spanish: "Ah, *señor*, so we meet again. You did me a favor the other night, albeit inadvertently. Perhaps you have come so I may return it?"

I sat down and drew a deep breath. My knowledge of Spanish is barely adequate. I can inquire courteously the direction of the men's room, I can order a drink, and conduct an intelligible conversation provided my auditor has patience and is not adverse to a constant and dogged use of the present tense.

Hence, this interview was going to be something of a task. I had to acquaint Mercado with the principal facts of the case and also induce him to handle it for, say, two thousand pesos, so that I could pocket the rest.

While I was pulling myself mentally together, Mercado picked up a glass, wiped it out with his handkerchief and filled it with water from a sealed carafe. He held it up to the light and squinted.

"Do you know," he said, "that in a drop of distilled water there are, on an average, six billion, three hundred million bacteria? In distilled water, mark you! Think how many there must be in ordinary liquid!"

He clucked as if resigning himself in the face of such overwhelming peril. He drank the water with his eyes half closed, as if imbibing a cup prepared by Lucrezia Borgia.

He put the glass down. "Disease," he said. "We must fight it, *señor*. You will note there is not a pillow in this apartment. I have no nests for germs. Health is a gift from heaven. We must devote our lives—"

"*Sí, sí,*" I said hastily. I gathered that germs were a subject to which the Señor Mercado was willing to devote himself with larynx and tongue for long periods of time. It was better that I cut him off now. I drew another breath and dived into my limited Spanish vocabulary with both hands.

"*Señor,*" I said, "are you interested in making two thousand pesos?"

His reaction was unexpected and entirely un-Mexican. "Money," he said musingly. "Do you have any idea how many germs there are on the average peso note?"

"Billions," I said quickly, "and billions. But, *señor,* I have a case for you. I am here to call upon you in your professional capacity. This is a murder case. I believe I can get you a fee of two thousand pesos for your services."

Mariano Mercado sighed. Since I refused to discuss bacteria, he reluctantly came to the matter in hand.

"Very well," he said. "What is it you have to tell me?"

I gave it to him, slowly and in detail. I told him how Fuller and Diaz had been arguing over the zinc concession, of how Bob Leftworth, a business rival of Fuller's, who was also in the country, seemed to have the inside track with Diaz. The papers were ready for signing. Diaz had kept the appointment at Fuller's place to listen to a last-minute appeal.

Moreover, I told him what I had already told the incredulous Fuller about the brawl I had heard in the library, when young Jerry Walters threatened Diaz. I told him further that it looked as if Walters had bribed José to lie and that, under the circumstances, no one would believe me.

When I had concluded he regarded me thoughtfully. "So," he said, "I am to get two thousand pesos for a murder case in which you already tell me the name of the murderer."

"Right. But, as I said, I'll be considered an interested witness. My evidence isn't worth anything. Now that I've told you this, it should be easy for you to trap Walters."

He nodded. "I shall accept the commission—on one condition."

"Which is?"

"That I am not required to enter any unsanitary place—that I am not, in the course of my duties, exposed to any perilous bacteriological situation."

"Done," I said. "Perhaps you will now accompany me to the scene of the crime?"

He nodded again and stood up. He slipped on a sweater and put on his coat. His suit today, I observed, was a restrained tan, the color of an autumn leaf in a dry country. His tie was a cerise noose tied so tightly it reminded me of the silken cord they used to hang peers with in England.

He gathered up some of the less lethal-appearing bottles on the desk and dropped them into his pocket. He buttoned his coat tightly in order to keep out the chilling Mexican air whose temperature at the moment was exactly seventy-two.

WE WENT down into the street and hailed a taxicab. I gave the driver Fuller's address.

"All you have to do," I told him, "is tell Fuller through me, of course, that you accept the case and the fee. Then it is a simple matter of watching Walters carefully, searching his things, perhaps, or threatening him into a confession. It is as easy as that. Probably the easiest money you ever earned, eh?"

I looked at him to find out he wasn't paying me the slightest attention. His gaze was directed to a fat Indian woman in the street whose face was covered with black blemishes.

"*Pinta,*" he said with a shudder. "The germs get under the skin and are impossible to get out again. Do you know how many germs are living in that woman's body?"

"Billions," I said. "Trillions. But for God's sake, will you realize we are engaged upon a murder case?"

"It is an interesting fact," he said, "that the bacteria in the human body do not die until long after the person has ceased living. You see, the germ life…."

I gave up then. For the rest of the journey I listened to a gloomy discourse of death, bacteria and the helplessness of man upon an earth so thickly populated with invisible microbes.

We arrived at Fuller's house to find that the coppers had been and gone, bearing with them the corpse of Genaro Diaz. Fuller, Ruth, and Jerry Walters were in the study. Walters was a young, handsome, dark-haired lad with features which even his mother would not have classified as strong. At the moment, I was pleased to note, he seemed nervous.

He sat on the edge of the couch and kept smoothing his hair nervously. Ruth Fuller was at his side and as I entered she shot a hostile glance at me.

"What do you mean by saying Jerry killed Diaz?" she demanded in a flat, cold voice. "You know damned well he can't speak Spanish. Dad told me what you'd said."

"All right," I said wearily. "All right. I'm rather tired of being branded a liar for today. May I present the Señor Mariano Mercado, *detective particular?* Let's see at whom he points the finger of suspicion."

Mercado beamed around the room and the sun came in through the patio doors and bounced brilliantly off his white teeth.

"All right," said Fuller. "Have you made the necessary financial arrangements with him? Have you told him I am willing to spend ten thousand pesos?"

"I have."

"O.K. Let's acquaint him with the facts. Then, Latham, you phone the papers and announce that, shocked and grieved by the death of my friend, Diaz, I have hired a private investigator to bring the murderer to justice."

"I can call now, then," I said. "I've already acquainted him with the facts of the case."

"Wait a minute," said Walters excitedly. "Mr. Fuller, if Latham has told only his biased version of the matter, God knows what garbled report Señor Mercado has. We must tell him the truth."

"Naturally," said Ruth, her eyes venomously upon me, "Mr. Latham has told Mr. Mercado that Jerry is guilty."

I shrugged my shoulders. "All right," I said. "What do you want to tell him?"

"Wait a minute," cried Walters again. "Don't let Latham do the interpreting. Heaven knows how he'll distort what you say, Mr. Fuller!"

I sighed. I seemed to have quite a reputation among those present.

Harvey Fuller kept his eyes on me and nodded slowly. "Of course, you're right, Jerry," he said. "We'd be fools to trust Latham, who seems bent on seeing you hang. I'll send out for an interpreter." He sighed again. "This language problem is such a damned nuisance. Now, if Mercado only knew a few words of English we could understand each other, somehow."

During this hearty fraternal dialogue, Mariano Mercado had sat quietly, blinking around the room. Now he straightened up suddenly.

"Telegony," he said amazingly. "Continuum. Uxorious. Viviparous."

WE ALL stared at him. Fuller took the cigar from his mouth, said, "Huh," and put it back again.

"You see," said Mariano Mercado in infinitely better English than was spoken by anyone in the room, "you were wrong, Mr. Fuller. If I knew only a few words of English, you would not necessarily understand them. For instance, you do not understand the words I have just spoken. However, most fortunately, I command other, simpler words of your language. I understand them, too. The fee you are offering, I believe, is ten thousand pesos?"

I clapped my hand to my head and was aware of a strong current of hate against Mariano Mercado.

"You double-crosser," I yelled. "Why didn't you tell me you spoke English?"

Mercado flashed me his snowiest smile. "I do not recall that you asked me."

Fuller slapped his hand upon his knee and burst into coarse laughter.

"This is terrific. How much of that ten thousand did you offer him, Latham?"

"Two thousand," said Mercado. "However, I agree that Mr. Latham is entitled to a commission for bringing the case to my attention. Moreover, I am most grateful for the use of his hat the other evening. I shall be no less generous than Mr. Latham. I now offer him two thousand pesos of the ten as a commission and for his services which I may need while engaged upon the case."

I opened my mouth to utter a sharp refusal. Then I shut it again. In my present financial condition, two thousand pesos was not precisely alfalfa. Moreover, I was morally certain that Jerry Walters had murdered Diaz. And if I were able, directly or indirectly, to pin the crime upon him, it would afford me a vast amount of satisfaction.

Now that it was established that Mariano Mercado, *detective particular*, spoke an excellent grade of English, the room was filled with eager babble. Ruth, Walters and Fuller began simultaneously to give their opinions of the reasons and methods of the death of Genaro Diaz. They were still unintelligibly at it when José opened the door and Bob Leftworth came into the room.

The prime difference between Leftworth and Fuller was that in the case of the former his wealth had not run to fat. Leftworth was tall, lean and almost cadaverous. His black eyes glanced mockingly at Fuller as he said: "Hello."

Fuller nodded. "I thought I'd left you at the Foreign Club."

"You did," said Leftworth in a slow drawl. "But right after our little chat, I heard an amazing thing. I heard that Diaz had been murdered in your house. Do you think the Better Business Association would approve such tactics?"

Fuller glared at him, then said icily: "I have excellent evidence that I am not involved. Moreover, I am paying a stiff fee to a private detective to look into the case for me. Now, is there anything else you want to ask, Señor Mercado?"

Mercado shrugged his shoulders and stood up. "I think not. I shall get in touch with you when necessary."

He bowed and strode out of the room. I looked after him with frank envy.

First, he was going to collect a cold eight thousand pesos, provided he paid me the two thousand he had promised. Second, I had thrown the case in his lap by telling him even before he had seen Fuller that, without doubt, Walters had killed Diaz. Never had a *detective particular* had such a windfall without working.

I spent the afternoon losing thirty pesos out at the Hippodrome Racetrack, and in the late afternoon returned to my hotel. I ate a bad dinner and spent a somewhat sleepless night. On second thought, I came to the conclusion that perhaps Mariano Mercado wasn't going to have as easy a time as I had first thought.

There was no evidence against Walters save mine. No one seemed willing to believe me. What was needed, I decided, was some more and conclusive evidence with which I had no connection at all. I thought about this for a long time before I finally went to sleep.

CHAPTER FOUR

THE AMBER SANDS
OF ACAPULCO

THE FOLLOWING morning, I attended to a few more or less personal matters, then went to call on Mariano Mercado. I waited in his sterilized office until he finished gargling in the bathroom. He emerged after a few moments, bowed to me and sat down at his desk.

"Well," I asked. "Any progress? Have you grilled Walters yet?"

Mercado shook his head. "I shall have to handle this in my own way," he said. "Now, who is the least likely suspect in the case?"

"That's easy," I said. "Leftworth. He was a cinch to get the mine concession if Diaz had lived. He's a cinch not to, now."

"Good," said Mercado. "We shall investigate Leftworth first."

I blinked at him. This seemed even less logical than his dread of germs.

"You see," said Mercado, "I usually investigate the least likely suspect first. It saves time."

This made even less sense than his first statement. I said so.

"It's an elimination process," went on Mercado, his tone implying I was rather stupid not to see it. "Usually, it is simpler to eliminate the least likely suspects. Then you can really go to work on those that remain."

I lit a cigarette and let him see that the bewilderment on my face had not abated.

"On the other hand," he continued, "if you start with a likely suspect who proves to be innocent, you spend so much time checking every angle that it enables the least likely suspect—always supposing he is guilty—to take warning and cover up. And if the most likely suspect is actually guilty, as he usually is, it takes very little time to get around to investigating him, for the check on the least likely suspect is usually over in a few hours."

By this time I was reeling. "Look," I said, "I never thought I'd say this, but I think I'd rather listen to you discuss bacteria."

"Would you?" said Mercado brightly. "Consider this: Would you prefer to be bitten by a boy or a dog? Do you know that there are more variegated germs in the human mouth than in that of any other animal? Consider this, *amigo*."

"I flatly refuse to consider it," I said. "I also refuse to consider that Bob Leftworth killed Diaz. I've told you once that Walters is the murderer. I tell you again. I insist you search his hotel room before anything else."

"Why?"

"Because you may find some evidence which corroborates what I've already told you."

Mercado looked thoughtful. He took a complicated atomizer from a desk drawer and sprayed his throat. Then he said: "Why are you so anxious to convict Walters? Are the reasons personal, or have you an overdeveloped sense of justice?"

It was a fair question—one which I had deliberately refrained from asking myself. Reluctantly, I considered it.

It was true I had once been engaged to Ruth Fuller, that Jerry Walters had superseded me. That, of course, was a blow to my ego. I was certain, however, it was nothing more. I was sure I no longer loved Ruth, unsure that I ever had. She was spoiled and selfish and was no wife for a man whose income was vastly less than her own.

But, despite these facts, I assuredly did not like Walters. And I did not like Fuller. I would shed no tears if the potential son-in-law, of whom Fuller approved, were shunted off to a Mexican prison for twenty-odd years.

And in addition to all this, I was positive Walters was the killer. I had heard what I had heard even if no one believed me. Like every other normal person, I had an aversion to murder and murderers. Walters was guilty and he should be tried for his offense.

Lastly, Walters' conviction would absolve me of the charge of lying in an attempt to frame a man I didn't like. I listed all these reasons to Mercado, and urged him once more to search Walters' hotel room before he did anything else.

"How?" said Mercado. "How am I to get into his hotel room?"

That was a question I had never expected to hear from any detective, official, private, or for that matter, *particular.* My opinion of Mariano Mercado dropped several inches.

"There are many simple, tried-and-true methods," I told him. "Perhaps the easiest is merely to ask for the key. It's a big hotel and Walters has only been there a week. Certainly the clerks don't know him."

"I am a Mexican," said Mercado. "They will certainly know I'm not a New Yorker whose name is Walters."

"True enough. I'll get the key for you."

Mercado sighed and stood up. "Very well, since you are so damned insistent."

FIRST, I checked circumspectly, discovered Walters was having lunch at Fuller's house, then we took a taxi to the hotel. Ten minutes later we were up in Walters' room.

I figured I had done enough of Mercado's work for the day. I lounged by the window while he gave the room a frisk which was surprisingly professional. However, he found nothing. He completed his task, looked over at me and shrugged. On the table by the window lay four books.

Catching Mercado's eye I glanced down at them significantly.

He paid no attention to me. I sighed and wondered how the devil he ever made a living as a private detective.

"Well," he said, "I trust you're satisfied. Obviously, there's nothing here."

I stared at the books again. There was a Prescott on Mexico, a guide to the city, a recently published novel and an English-Spanish dictionary. Still Mariano Mercado paid me no heed. I tried a more direct approach.

"Did you look through these books? People often hide things in books."

"Hardly confessions of murder," said Mercado. "At least I never heard of it being done."

Nevertheless he picked up one of the books and riffled its pages. He repeated the process until he came to the dictionary. Then his eye caught something on one of its pages. He thumbed through it more slowly, then dropped it in his pocket.

"Well," I said, trying to keep the eagerness out of my tone, "find anything?"

He regarded me with an odd expression. He shook his head and said slowly: "Maybe. I'm not quite sure."

I shrugged and let it go at that. It seemed to me that by now he should have made up his mind about the identity of Diaz' killer. But if he wanted to mull over it for a few hours it wouldn't make a great deal of difference.

We left the room and went down into the lobby. I accompanied Mariano Mercado back to his office. I noticed that he was silent and thoughtful. Why, I didn't know. From his point of view, everything should be as plain as a bayonet by this time.

He left me to pay the cab and went up the stairs into his flat. I was held up some time while the driver canvassed the stores on each side of the street seeking change for a twenty-peso note. As he finally counted the change into my palm, Mercado came dashing out of the building and sprang into the cab again.

Wonderingly, I climbed in, too. Mercado shot a Spanish address at the driver, then turned to me.

"Grew's dead!" he said. "Murdered. Happened less than an hour ago. There was a message from Fuller in the house."

"Grew?" I said, puzzled. I was sure I knew all the angles on the death of Diaz, but I couldn't figure Grew in it at all.

Albert Grew was a bookish sort of lad who had come to Mexico as an assistant to the commercial attache of the Embassy. He was something of a linguist and, liking the country, he had quit his job and set up in business for himself as a Spanish teacher to Americans and Englishmen.

I had met him a couple of times and quite probably would have forgotten his name had it not been for the fact that Fuller had engaged him for lessons, had been due to take the first one on the day that Diaz was killed.

But if Walters had killed the Mexican, and I firmly believed he had, I could see no motive for his killing Grew.

TEN MINUTES later, we disembarked again in a street of moderately priced stores and apartments. In front of us loomed a tremendous hardware store. Over its plate glass windows was a wide, black board upon which had been nailed enormous gilt convex letters spelling out with Castillian pride the owner's name: JUAN MONDRAGON & CIA., S.A.

Mercado left me to pay the hack for the second time and entered the building. I followed a moment later in time to see his dapper little figure disappear through a doorway on the first landing. A moment later I found myself in Grew's living room.

It was a comfortably furnished room, its walls lined with bookcases, filled and apparently often read. But at the moment it was in chaotic disorder. Obviously, it had been searched. On the couch something large and irregular lay motionless beneath a sheet. Lounging against the wall was an indolent copper. He nodded at Mercado. Obviously he was a policeman too indifferent to his job to resent the intrusion of a *detective particular.*

They went into rapid Spanish which I didn't even try to follow. After some ten minutes of it, Mercado sat down and lit a cigarette. He seemed troubled. His mind seemed so far away that I'm sure a germ could have sneaked up on him completely unobserved.

"Well," I said, "what happened?"

Mercado shrugged. "It's rather bewildering," he said. "Grew was knifed. His landlady found him a couple of hours ago. He was still alive when she arrived and the room, as you see, was ransacked."

"Then," I said, "he named his killer?"

"No," said Mercado. "He only uttered two words. He spoke them three times."

"What were they?"

"I'm not sure. But they apparently were English. He said, 'amber sands,' three times. Of course, this was heard only by the landlady who speaks no English so we can't be sure."

"Amber sands?" I repeated. "Have the coppers any theory?"

"They have, as usual. They checked and found out that Grew went down to Acapulco for the swimming whenever he had the chance. He was crazy about the beach. They think—"

"I get it," I said. "He was delirious. He was raving about that terrific beach at Acapulco. The amber sands, get it? It's obvious."

Mercado shook his hands doubtfully. "I'm not so sure," he said. "Besides, there's something else."

"Which is?"

He stood up abruptly and I could hear the arsenal of bottles rattle in his pockets. "There was a strange car parked outside for about a half hour before Grew was found stabbed. It had an American license plate. No one, however, got the number."

"My God!" I said excitedly. "What kind of car? What model?"

"Pontiac coupe. 1940."

"Click!" I yelled. "I told you. That's Walters' car."

Mercado nodded without surprise. "I am not amazed."

"Neither am I," I said grimly. "This proves I'm no liar. Moreover, it proves Walters the killer. He killed Diaz, I know that. He probably killed Grew because maybe Grew taught him some Spanish, probably told him what to say to Diaz. Walters was afraid if Grew said so, everyone would know I wasn't lying. Now do you get it?"

Mariano Mercado paced the floor. Obviously, he wasn't listening to me. I became annoyed. There seemed to be a tacit conspiracy to make certain that Jerry Walters literally got away with murder. Mercado stopped pacing abruptly and said: "Leftworth has a house in Cuernavaca, hasn't he?"

"Yes. But, for God's sake, why? What's Leftworth got to do with it? Are you still pursuing your least likely suspect theory?"

"Perhaps. Anyway, let's go out and call on him."

"Are you crazy?" I yelled. "Go and pinch Walters. My God—"

"You may pinch Walters," he said, walking to the door. "I'm going to Cuernavaca."

He strode into the hall, while I glared after him. I had about as much authority to pinch Walters as I had to mobilize the Mexican army. Finally, I shrugged my shoulders and followed him.

A FEW moments later the taxi Mercado had hired raced through the suburbs of Mexico City, past Xochimilco to the curving, dangerous mountain road to Cuernavaca. We rode in silence, Mercado apparently occupied in thought, I in sullen anger at his stubborn stupidity.

Then some fifteen kilometers out of town, we both spotted the car ahead simultaneously.

"That's it!" I yelled as I saw the coupe with the New York license plate. "Walters is trying to make a getaway. We'll nail him dead to rights."

Mariano Mercado paid no attention to me. He leaned forward in his seat and instructed the driver to pass the car ahead. As we forged past the Pontiac on the narrow road both of us peered intently out the open window.

There was but one person in the car and it was not Walters. A thin, swarthy figure sat at the wheel. There were two ugly, pale scars, reminiscent of knife wounds, on his face. He did not look up as we passed.

We shot ahead. Mercado spoke to the driver. "Keep about half a kilometer ahead of that car," he said, then lapsed once more into thoughtful silence.

I considered for a moment, then said: "It's still easy. Walters hired a thug. A killer. That's him in the car."

"You're half right," said Mercado. "Morelos is a thug."

"You mean that guy at the wheel? Do you know him?"

He nodded. "Every copper in Mexico knows him. Moreover, they know he's a killer. But they've never been able to prove it. He lives in a well known hotel and more or less defies the entire Federal Police."

I sank back in my seat well satisfied. Everything seemed to fit in perfectly once more.

"Though I know Morelos both by sight and reputation," said Mercado musingly, "I doubt that he knows me. Perhaps it would be well to get into the car with him. Perhaps we might find something in the car or, if he is unsuspicious of us, trap him into a damaging admission."

I sighed and shrugged my shoulders. Mariano Mercado, true to the tradition of the storybook detective was not going to do it the easy way. I had explained that Diaz murder to him. I had explained the killing of Grew. Yet Mercado persisted in playing Sherlock Holmes to my irritated Doctor Watson.

He leaned forward again and spoke to the driver. Some pesos passed hands. A moment later the taxi slewed across the road, effectively blocking traffic, and stopped. Mercado climbed out. I followed him. A moment later the coupe came around the curve. Its brakes screeched. It halted a few feet from us.

Mercado showed all his teeth in his most ingratiating smile. He opened the door of the coupe and said to Morelos: "Will you aid us? Our cab has broken down. Will you take us to the nearest gas station where we may get assistance?"

Morelos was by no means cordial. But even before he had finished his sentence, Mercado was already in the car. I squeezed in beside him as the cab driver pushed his car over to the side of the road to give us clearance.

The coupe started. Morelos grunted but did not speak and we went on. I glanced swiftly around the car. There was certainly nothing in it which might be considered a clue, but considering the evidence Mercado already had, I couldn't see that it made any difference.

I looked at the speedometer. The needle was close to fifty which was a dangerous speed over this narrow and constantly winding road. Then I looked at Morelos. He stared straight ahead and his jaw moved rhythmically as he chewed tobacco.

Morelos took his eyes off the road for a moment and spat tobacco juice out the window. The wind was most unfavorable. A stream of brown saliva was promptly hurled back into the car. Three drops landed on Mariano Mercado's chin. The rest enhanced the glorious beige of his tie.

Mercado uttered a shriek, half of rage, half of fear. "*¡Válgame Dios!*" he cried. "Are you mad, *hombre?* Do you know the bacteriological contents of this stuff?"

He scraped his face with his handkerchief. He was gray with fright. Morelos grinned at him.

"It won't hurt you," he said in Spanish. "Even a little more won't hurt."

He opened his mouth and turned again to the window to expel more tobacco juice. Mercado uttered a howl. He reached across me and opened the door of the coupe. He shoved against me with all his might. He knocked me out into space and followed a second later himself.

IN THE instant that I was hurtling above the shoulder of the road I remembered that when I had last read the speedometer it had registered fifty. It came to me that when I landed I was going to be a hospital case. It was all very well for Mercado to prefer a broken neck to a few germs on his chin, but I was most indignant that he had forced me to share his views in the matter.

I landed alive, though with a good deal of skin clipped from my nose and knees. I got painfully to my feet, to see the coupe round a bend in the distance and with indignation overwhelming me.

I turned around to face Mercado. Apparently he was unscathed. He was spraying some sort of disinfectant from an atomizer all over his face.

"You idiot," I yelled. "Are you crazy? We might have been killed. Do you know we were going fifty miles an hour?"

He lowered the atomizer and stared at me. *"Dios,"* he said, "fifty miles an hour! I'm glad you said that. Fifty miles an hour and the amber sands of Acapulco. *Dios,* there's the entire case in our laps."

"Did you land on your head?" I asked bitterly. "What jargon are you talking now?"

He regarded me with mockery. "I am speaking English," he said haughtily. "If you knew your own language as well as I do, you might understand me."

I looked around me and saw nothing but mountains. "How the devil do we get out of here?"

"There's a gas station with a phone about three kilos away. We'll walk there. On the way I shall tell you what I expect from you tomorrow."

We trudged along the road.

"You will call Fuller," said Mercado. "You will tell him to have everyone assembled at his house at noon."

"Who's everyone?"

"Fuller, his daughter, Walters, Leftworth and yourself. I shall have the police bring Morelos along under escort. If they think I can pin something on him, I'm sure they will cooperate."

"What the devil have all these people to do with the two murders? Why do you need them to charge Walters and possibly Morelos with murder?"

"The connection of the others," said Mariano Mercado, "I shall tell you tomorrow. You already know your own connection in the affair."

He stared at me so steadily that I reddened beneath his scrutiny. How much he knew I wasn't sure. Neither was I certain as to whether Mariano Mercado, *detective particular*, was something of a pompous dolt, or a very shrewd little package, indeed.

CHAPTER FIVE

DOUBLECROSS— LATIN STYLE

IT SEEMED that the clan had already gathered when Mercado and I arrived at Fuller's. Mercado looked about the room, achieved a Renaissance bow and showed his enviable teeth. I nodded brusquely and sat down.

I took stock of the audience. Fuller sat behind his desk, a cigar in one hand and a Cuba libre in the other. He looked sleek and smug, rather like a fat cat who has stumbled across a derailed milk train. The reason for this was clear enough.

He fully expected that Mariano Mercado was about to unmask the killer of Genaro Diaz. That done, he would phone every daily paper in town, take several modest bows and ingratiate himself with a government which was on the verge of handing him a million dollar concession.

Over on the sofa, Ruth Fuller and Jerry Walters sat huddled together. Walters, I thought, seemed a trifle nervous. Ruth was defiantly belligerent, as if tacitly challenging Mercado to utter a single derogatory word about her fiancé. They ignored me completely.

On the other side of the room, sprawling in a leather chair, was Bob Leftworth. His angular figure was bent at the knees, the hips and the shoulders. He was giving his wholehearted attention to Mercado, as if trying to look through the latter's ebony eyes and read what was in his mind.

Morelos and a copper completed the assembly. Morelos stood scowling against the wall. The scar on his face was livid and his frown was volcanic. His arms were folded and he wore the expression of a man who was prepared to fight if things went against him. Mercado had informed me that he understood enough English to follow the proceedings. The copper who had brought him lounged at Morelos' side and appeared mildly bored by the entire proceedings.

Mariano Mercado took a dominant position in the center of the room, looked about, counted heads, and said: "Where is your *criado*, José?"

I sighed and shook my head. There were doubtful moments when I believed that Mariano Mercado was not very bright. I knew who had killed Diaz and Grew. Moreover, I knew that unless Mercado's forefathers were of the Mexican branch of the Juke family, he knew, too. He had all the evidence he needed. Yet he was asking for the harmless José who, I was certain, had nothing more to do with either killing than Camacho himself.

Fuller, however, appeared to find nothing odd in the request. He yanked the bell pull on the wall and a moment later José shuffled into the room, leaving the door open behind him. Mercado waved him to the wall alongside the bored policeman. Then he glanced at the open door and shuddered.

"Valgame Dios!" he cried in anguished tones. "Close that door! Shall we all die in an oxygen tent with pneumonia?"

The temperature was a steady seventy-two. There was not a ghost of a zephyr stirring. Nevertheless, I humored him. I got up and closed the door. As I took my seat again, I saw the thoughtful expression that had crawled into his eyes. I knew what was coming.

"Of course," he said pontifically, "it has never been definitely established that the common cold is caused by a germ. However, all researches indicate—"

"Unless," cut in Leftworth sharply, "you are about to argue that Diaz and Grew were killed by the common cold, suppose you drop the subject and get on with what you have to say about murder. I'm a busy man."

I GRINNED at the crestfallen expression on Mercado's face. He looked like a garrulous mother who has been cut off in the middle of her favorite baby anecdote.

"Yes, yes," said Fuller, with heavy good-fellowship, "let's get down to business, señor. It will be most gratifying to me to have been an instrument in the solution of Diaz' killing, even though he was opposed to granting me valuable concessions."

"Oh, no," said Mercado blandly, "you are wrong there, *señor.* Genaro Diaz was going to give you your concessions. On the very day he was killed he was about to tell you so."

Fuller blinked. I could see what faith he had in Mercado oozing out of him. He had spent days and nights arguing with Diaz about those zinc mines. But Diaz had been adamant—the mines were to go to Leftworth.

"Well," said Jerry Walters, "this certainly is a new angle. I—"

"If the remainder of Mr. Mercado's theory is as sound as this one," said Ruth, "I'm afraid we're all wasting our time."

Mercado looked at her reproachfully. He sighed heavily, said: "It is a most deplorable case."

Even Fuller was looking leery now. It appeared as if Mariano Mercado, *detective particular,* was stalling. The only statement he had put forward—that Diaz was about to award the zinc concessions to Fuller—was most dubious, and beyond that and an aborted lecture on the common cold, he had said precisely nothing.

"Yes," went on Mercado, "the whole case is a history of deplorable doublecrosses, all of which happened because Genaro Diaz was a man of honor and integrity. There has been a vast quantity of lying, illuminated by some fragments of truth."

"Well," put in Ruth, "Jerry told the truth throughout—when he said he wasn't in the house, that he didn't speak Spanish, that he didn't use threatening words to Diaz in the library."

She glared at me when she finished as if challenging me to reiterate my story. I shook my head and silently cursed Mercado. How he could let that speech go unchallenged in view of the evidence I knew he had, was beyond me. I had just about reached the conclusion that he was a brainless charlatan, when he said: "I fear you are wrong again, *señorita*. It was the Señor Latham who spoke the truth when he said he overheard your fiancé speaking Spanish in the library."

I drew a deep breath and my faith in Mariano Mercado returned. Of course, I told myself, he had the answers. He had been stalling because of his Latin sense of the dramatic, to create suspense. I sat back and waited for him to point an accusing finger at Jerry Walters.

Fuller looked worried, Ruth apoplectic, and Walters uneasy. Morelos retained his stone face, but I thought I detected a gleam of satisfaction in Leftworth's eye.

Ruth Miller slapped her hand on the arm of the couch. "You are a fool!" she said angrily. "Jerry doesn't know a word of Spanish. Not a single word."

Mercado bowed politely. "This time, *señorita*," he said, "you are half right. I am not a fool. Yet it is true that Señor Walters does not know a word of Spanish."

At this point all of us looked as blank as an unused note book. Fuller blinked, then said very slowly, like a man who is striving to make himself thoroughly clear: "You say Walters threatened Diaz in the library in Spanish? You also admit that Walters does not know a single word of the language?"

"That is it, *señor*," said Mercado. "I am glad to see you understand so rapidly."

THIS TIME, Fuller's jaw actually dropped. He understood neither rapidly nor in any other matter. Nor, for that matter, did anyone else. I gave up all over again. I reverted to my opinion that Mercado would never have passed the Japanese army intelligence test. It was Ruth who voiced the thought that was in each of our heads.

"How in the name of heaven," she demanded, "could Latham have heard Jerry talking Spanish when he can't speak a word of it?"

Mariano Mercado sighed heavily, as if the density of his audience was too much for him.

"I didn't say he couldn't speak Spanish. Anyone can *speak* Spanish if it is written down for them. I merely said that Walters didn't *know* any Spanish. He doesn't. He didn't have the slightest idea of what he was saying."

Ruth's annoyance at Mercado evaporated immediately. It was replaced by a look of something approaching awe. Walters registered something between acute worry and vast relief. Once again I lifted my estimation of Mercado. I waited confidently for him to produce his next statement which I was sure would be conclusive evidence.

"You mean," said Fuller, "that Walters read those Spanish words to Diaz—that Latham really heard him say them?"

"Exactly, *señor.*"

Fuller's bewilderment in no wise decreased. Glancing over at Morelos, I noted he was staring at Mercado. His expression was not pleasant. Mercado's gaze was directed out the window. Before he spied some germ life and embarked upon a harangue, I decided to take matters in hand myself.

"Look," I said, "it's simple. It would have been much simpler if you'd believed me in the first place when I told you what I'd overheard in the library. Walters was sore because Diaz was paying attention to Ruth, who, for reasons of policy couldn't very well rebuff him. So Walters, speaking no Spanish, looked up the words he wanted in the dictionary, copied them out, and read them off to Diaz, or maybe Grew helped him. Diaz got sore, pulled a gun or something, so Walters yanked a knife off the wall and killed him. There it is, with no more hocus-pocus."

"That's a lie," cried Ruth Fuller, in a tone which was perilously close to hysteria. "A damnable dirty lie!"

"I was framed," cried Walters. "I can explain everything. I never copied—"

"Shut up," said Ruth, suddenly self-possessed.

Mariano Mercado flashed his teeth at me and inquired sweetly: "And how do you know all this, Señor Latham?"

"I know because I saw that dictionary in Walters' room before you did. I saw what words were underlined. They were the same words I heard Walters address to Diaz."

Mercado's white teeth vanished as his lips closed and he regarded me severely. "I know quite well you saw that dictionary before I did."

"So what? And how can you know? I never told you."

"No, you didn't. But you *did* underline those words yourself."

There was a deadly silence in the room. Despite all my efforts I could feel the hot color surging to my cheeks. I looked guilty as hell and it didn't make matters any better that I was aware of it.

Walters stared at me, horrified. "My God," he said, "so it was you who framed me! I thought all the time it was Grew."

"Are you trying to say," asked Fuller hopefully, "that Latham really murdered Diaz, then tried somehow to pin it on Walters?"

To my unutterable relief, Mercado shook his head. "No," he said. "All Latham did was to mark up Walters' Spanish-English dictionary. For that he may be forgiven since he really believed Walters was the killer. He actually thought Walters a murderer who was about to get away with his murder. So he tried to bring about justice by framing him."

"For God's sake," said Bob Leftworth, "did we come here to listen to a solution to the mystery or merely to hear it get more jumbled up than ever?"

"I will simplify it for you," said Mercado. "Grew murdered Diaz. Grew then double-crossed his partner and José doublecrossed Grew."

"Great heavens!" said Fuller. "Is this simplification?"

"We will take it slowly," said Mercado rather condescendingly. "On the day of the murder, Grew learns that Diaz will be in this house. He learns, further, that Fuller will be delayed in meeting him. He has prepared for this day. He has obtained José as a confederate at, of course, a price."

I STILL didn't know where Mariano Mercado, *detective particular,* was headed, but one glance at the sudden ash which colored José's coffee-hued features was enough to convince me he was moving in the direction of truth.

"Now, Grew also has been called by Walters who wants to take Spanish lessons. On the morning of the murder Grew phones Walters, tells him he'll give him his lesson in Fuller's library since he already has an appointment later with Fuller for another lesson. Walters, who has the run of the house here, thought nothing of it and arrived at the appointed hour."

It hit me then. True, it was several hours after it had hit Mariano Mercado, but at least it was before anyone else in the room had figured it.

"I see it," I announced. "José admitted Grew, but later denied it. Grew knifed Diaz, dragged the body into the lavatory, then awaited the arrival of Walters. He handed Walters a piece of paper upon which was typed some Spanish. He told Walters some cock-and-bull story about the importance of a correct accent and told him to read the words aloud. Walters did and I heard him."

"Which was accidental and not particularly important," said Mercado. "But the fact that José heard him was the paramount point."

"But José said he heard nothing," said Fuller.

"He also said that Walters had not been in the house, that Grew had not been in the house, and that Grew had telephoned saying he couldn't come. All these statements are lies."

Now I had completely lost it again. "But why?" I asked. "Why is José doing all this lying?"

"José had been well bribed. He was to be the witness who swore he heard Walters threatening Diaz. Naturally, when he confronted Walters with the evidence, Walters would tell the truth. Grew would deny it. And José would deny that Grew had ever been in the house. Walters' word would never, under the circumstances, be accepted."

"But, damn it all," yelled Fuller, "José also said that *Walters* wasn't in the house!"

Mercado nodded blandly. "That was the second dou-blecross," he said. "José's. José decided that Walters was a man of means. He could keep his original fee and could blackmail Walters for the rest of his life."

Ruth picked it up there. "That's true. Jerry told me all about it. We were afraid to tell the truth. José made his proposition, promised to keep his mouth shut if we'd accept it. We did. No one would have believed the truth."

Mariano Mercado nodded as if he had known these incredible facts all the time. I scratched my head and pondered. I was reluctant to give up the idea of Walters' guilt. And since I didn't see any motive for Grew's committing the crime, I clung to it doggedly for the time being.

"So you see," went on Mercado, "Grew waited for José to denounce Walters, as their plan called for, thus covering up for Grew for all time. But José was embarking on his own blackmail career. He made his deal with Walters and kept his mouth shut. Grew could say nothing without exposing his own hand, which, incidentally, was full, because he was working his own doublecross."

Fuller took his cigar from his mouth long enough to say interrogatively: "And the guy he crossed caught up with him and killed him?"

"Indirectly," said Mercado. "Actually, Morelos, here, killed him. *No hizo, valiente?*"

MORELOS' BREATH hissed sibilantly through his teeth. His muscles tightened and he looked as if he were about to spring. The bored copper came suddenly out of his lethargy and his hand went to his hip. To my surprise, I saw Leftworth's lips move as he said something inaudible. Morelos relaxed again.

Now, for the first time, I began to believe that I had been wrong from the beginning and Mariano Mercado right. But I still didn't see any motive for Grew as the killer. Moreover, if Morelos had slain Grew, which theory, under the circumstances, I was willing to accept, Walters might well have been the principal. After all, it was his car which we had found Morelos driving. I opened my mouth and said as much.

"*Dios mío,*" said Mariano Mercado mildly, "do you still believe that was Walters' car?"

"Well, wasn't it? It carried his license plates."

"It did. And it was a car of the same make, same model and same year. But it certainly wasn't Walters' car."

"Have you ever seen Walters' car?" I demanded.

"No."

"Then how the devil do you know whether it was or not?"

"It is elementary," said Mercado. "Has it never occurred to you that it would be most difficult to leap off a car that was traveling fifty miles an hour?"

"It has occurred to me. I still marvel that we weren't injured. But what the devil has that to do with the ownership of the car?"

"Everything," said Mercado. "Walters' car was bought in the United States. Its speedometer reads in miles, of course. The car we were in, the car which was supposed to be Walters', bore a Mexican speedometer, registering in kilometers. So, that figure fifty was really a kilometer reading. Actually, we were only going thirty miles an hour."

"You mean," I asked, "that someone deliberately tried to create the impression that the car was Walters' in order to frame him for the death of Grew? That someone obtained a car of the same make and model and put Walters' plates on it?"

"Exactly. The first frame had failed. Maybe, the second wouldn't. The killer wanted a suspect all ready for the police. He didn't want an investigation pushed too hard. It might have revealed the truth."

"Then I don't get it. What possible motive could Morelos have for killing Grew?"

"Money. He was paid for it."

CHAPTER SIX
OF AMPERSANDS
AND MURDER

THERE WAS a taut silence in the room, broken only by a sigh of Ruth Fuller's. Leftworth no longer slouched in his chair. He sat bolt upright, his air of bored insouciance gone. He stared at Mercado with an admixture of awe and menace.

"You have told us," said Fuller querulously, "that Grew killed Diaz and Morelos killed Grew. I am quite willing to accept this theory. But I would like to know why either of them killed anyone."

"Because," said Mercado, flashing his teeth in Leftworth's direction, "they were hired to do so."

"By whom?" said Leftworth between clenched teeth.

Mariano Mercado sighed, sat down on the arm of my chair and said: "By you, Señor Leftworth. Who else?"

Again Fuller and I looked doubtfully at Mariano Mercado. Of all the people in the room Leftworth seemed to have less reason than anyone to kill Diaz. Diaz' death had certainly snatched the mine concessions out of his hands. Fuller shook his head wearily and said as much.

Mariano Mercado remained unruffled. "I began this little talk," he said, "by saying that Genaro Diaz was a man of integrity. So he was. He was firmly convinced that granting the mine concessions to Leftworth would be of the greatest benefit to his country. However, he changed his mind as soon as he discovered Leftworth was a crook."

Morelos stirred. Both the copper and Leftworth shot hard glances at him. Leftworth said with artificial casualness: "I suppose you can prove all this?"

"Indeed," said Mercado. "Diaz had absolute proof of your chicanery. He obtained a document, I don't know how, which proved conclusively that you had bribed his men. You had also bribed the appraisers to under-value the mines in their report. You bribed Grew to kill Diaz who, you knew, had brought the document to show to Señor Fuller."

Fuller dropped his cigar. He smashed his fist on the desk and his face grew red. "God," he said, "it was Leftworth's call for me to see him immediately that made me late to meet Diaz here that day."

"Precisely," said Mercado. "Grew killed Diaz, took the incriminating document, but did not give it to Leftworth as per contract. He kept it for blackmail purposes, much the same as José kept his mouth shut in order to milk Walters."

"At last," I said, "it's easy. Then Leftworth hired Morelos to kill Grew and recover the document which was essential to keeping him out of trouble with the Mexican Government, also to put an end to Grew's blackmailing."

Leftworth moved in his chair. His eyes were hard. "I repeat," he said, "can you prove all this?"

"In time," said Mariano Mercado. "First, I should like to explain to Latham that it was no accident that we met Morelos in the car supposed to be Walters' on the Cuernavaca road. He was on his way back to Leftworth's with the car. Luckily for us he took his time after the murder. As soon as I realized that, I knew I had all the answers."

Mercado beamed at Leftworth and his teeth reflected the sunlight. "The document proves it for me," he said. "The document your hired killer, Morelos, couldn't find."

"Brilliant," said Fuller. "You have the paper?"

"I have it. Or rather, I have given it to the federal prosecutor."

Morelos came to life suddenly. "Where did you find it?" he asked. "Where, *cábron?*"

"In the amber sands," said Mercado.

I blinked. "You mean at Acapulco? You haven't been to the coast."

Mercado sighed. "It is strange that you Americans do not understand your own language. When Grew was dying he spoke, you thought, of the amber sands of Acapulco. He did not. What he said was *ampersand—*the *ampersand.* He was telling where the incriminating document would be found."

WE ALL looked blank. I asked the question which was in everyone's mind. "What the devil is an ampersand?"

"It is an English word," said Mercado reprovingly, "not a Spanish one. You will recall that directly outside the window of Grew's bedroom there is a sign, a gilded sign bearing the name of the store downstairs. It reads, 'Juan Mondragon & Cia.' That symbol representing the 'and' is called an ampersand."

"I've got it," I said. "Those were gilt letters, big and hollow, nailed to the black board. Reaching out his window Grew detached the ampersand, stuffed the paper in behind it for safekeeping."

"Right," said Mariano Mercado. "Of course, Morclos could not find it. But then," he added chidingly, "can you expect an illiterate Indio to know what an ampersand is if you educated gentlemen don't?"

I ran my fingers through my hair. Reluctantly I admitted to myself that Mariano Mercado was a far shrewder operator than I had thought. I recalled my efforts to pin the crime on Walters and was aware that my face grew uncomfortably red.

Across the room, I saw Morelos look inquiringly at Leftworth. Mercado, beaming like an actor taking a bow, did not notice it.

"So," he said, "Leftworth had to get that paper. True, he would lose the concessions anyway, but he would escape criminal prosecution. The evidence I have now and the fact that José will be required by the police to swear to the truth by the Saint of Guadaloupe, and, if necessary, by harsher methods will give us enough to jail the criminals in the case."

Leftworth stood up. He nodded to Morelos. Morelos' hand dived into his pocket. It reappeared an instant later holding a thirty-eight. The indolent copper at his side stared at it dully, then snapped his fingers like a man who remembers he has forgotten something. Which indeed he had—the minor matter of searching Morelos before he brought him in.

Morelos moved much faster than the policeman's brain cells. He swung the pistol with incredible speed, brought its barrel down on the officer's skull. The man's knees buckled and he sat gently upon the floor. Morelos' gun muzzle then covered the rest of us.

"Good," said Leftworth, his face pale and his lips set grimly. "Now, we will escort you all to another room in this house, a room in which there is not so much glass that you can break through. There we will lock you up in order to give us time to make our getaway."

"Venezuela," said Morelos in broken English. "I do not believe the police can touch us there."

At this moment, José fell to his knees, jabbering in Spanish. Half his prayer was devoted to repenting his awful sins, the other half to asking Guadaloupe to paralyze Morelos' trigger finger.

Ruth and Jerry Walters sat stunned on the couch. Fuller, who certainly was no United States Marine when it came to physical courage, had laid down his cigar and his drink and stared with frightened eyes across the room.

I considered myself something more of a rough and tumble fighter than the rest of them. However, I made no move. Morelos had the drop most certainly, and there was a desperate grimness about him that boded neither mercy nor consideration for any adversary.

"All right," said Leftworth. "Stand up. All of you. Turn your backs to us."

There was slow movement in the room. Then Mercado suddenly said: "I cannot permit the flouting of my country's laws."

WITH THAT he sprang into action like a puma. He snatched up Fuller's half-empty glass and hurled it at Morelos. At the same time he charged. He disposed of Leftworth, his patent leather shoe sinking into the American's groin. Morelos, half blinded by coca-cola and rum, fired wildly. The bullet entered the wall over my head.

In the next instant Mercado was clinging to Morelos' gun arm with one hand, while the other circled Morelos' brown throat. The two pressures, combined with a certain knowledge of jiujitsu leverage, brought Morelos to his knees, an expression of agony upon his face.

Again I marveled at Mariano Mercado. I had already admitted to myself that there were no bacteria addling his wits. But courage was a virtue I had hardly expected in him. He wasn't a big man and he seemed too concerned about his physical health to risk sudden extinction at the hands of a thug like Morelos.

Morelos slugged upward wildly at his adversary. But Mercado's slim brown fingers tightened about the other's throat like rusty springs. Morelos' eyes bulged. His jaw dropped open. A harsh, dry cough emanated from his throat full into Mariano Mercado's face.

Mercado sprang back as if a host of scorpions had jumped him. There was horror in his eyes and his face was the color of muddy milk. All the courage he had evinced a moment ago oozed from him like gas from a punctured balloon.

"*Dios mío,*" he cried and his voice shook with terror. "He has murdered me! He has assailed me with a billion germs!"

His hands rattled nervously in his pocket. He extracted two blue vials and a package of pills. Then, completely forgetting Morelos and the thirty-eight in his hand, he turned tail and fled ingloriously into the bathroom.

At this point I, who was vastly more afraid of a gun in the hand of a killer than of any germ life which ever existed, charged in. I was upon Morelos before he could recover. I wrenched the weapon from his grasp. I stood up, covering both Morelos and Leftworth, who had begun to stir on the floor.

"José," I said, "call the police."

José, who at this point was willing to do anything to ingratiate himself with anyone at all, obeyed.

I WAITED until the coppers arrived and took over. Then I sought out Mercado in the bathroom. He was still shaken, but apparently he had so dosed himself with antiseptics and preventives that he could again speak in a steady tone.

"Look," I said, "there's one thing I still want to know. How the devil did you know I underlined those words in the dictionary?"

He gave me a moderately realistic facsimile of his old flashing grin.

"It wasn't difficult," he said. "I knew you thought Walters was guilty. I knew you were breaking your neck to have me pin the killing on him. So I was rather prepared for what I found."

"Well, what the devil *did* you find?"

"You underlined all those words which you recalled Walters had spoken that morning. As you quoted his words to me, he had said, among other things: 'I am becoming angry,' and 'pay attention to me.' But, of course he said these things in Spanish. Thus for 'becoming' and 'pay' you used the verb *poner,* which means 'to put.' For in Spanish, as you well know, we say '*Put* attention to me' and 'it *puts* me angry.' No one who doesn't know Spanish would use those idioms. If Walters had looked up the words he wanted he would have marked literal English translations."

"I get it," I said. "So that was what gave you the idea that Walters was reading from script? "

He nodded. "Also that you had fixed the dictionary to fasten guilt on Walters."

Under his bland scrutiny, I blushed. "Well," I said lamely, "I'm glad it wasn't Walters. I'm even gladder I didn't succeed in pinning it on him since he was innocent."

"Forget it," said Mariano Mercado. "You aren't very bright, Latham, but I like you. I understand you haven't much cash. How would you like to carry on as my assistant?" I put out my hand. "It's a deal," I said. He ignored my hand and embraced me Latin fashion, kissing me on both cheeks.

He released me and said: "How do you stand with the Army back in the States?"

"A perfect 4F," I told him. "I had a touch of pneumonia a few months back. It developed into a slight case of tuberculosis. But it's cleared up nicely now. I—"

I broke off as I observed him staring at me as if I had suddenly metamorphosed into a rattlesnake. He pointed an accusing, hysterical forefinger at me.

"Tuberculosis!" he screamed. "And you let me kiss you? *Matador! Killer! Borgia!*"

I fled the room in the face of his wrath. As I closed the door behind me I heard the tinkle of medical equipment as Mariano Mercado once again prepared to march against the bacterial hosts.

THE VANISHING AMERICAN

WHEN A TOURIST DISAPPEARS FOR A FEW HOURS IN MEXICO, HE'S EITHER ENJOYING HIMSELF WITH THE FEMININE POPULATION OR SWILLING *HABANEROS* IN SOME *CANTINA*. IF ALBERT WELDON WAS DOING EITHER, HE COULDN'T HAVE BEEN ENJOYING HIMSELF VERY MUCH, HOWEVER, FOR THE MISSING MAN WAS A CORPSE—A CORPSE IN A TRUNK, WITH TWO THOUSAND PESOS AND A NOTE ADDRESSED TO MERCADO PINNED ON HIM SAYING, *"PLEASE FIND OUT WHO KILLED ME!"*

CHAPTER ONE
BLONDE FOR BREAKFAST

WHEN **I** left the hotel that morning, the Mexican sun blazed brightly down upon the city. This fact, however, did not prevent me from taking my raincoat along with me. Mexico's summer is also her rainy season. And it never drizzles up here on the plateau—it pelts down like tears in the Union League Club when Roosevelt is running for re-election.

I stopped off at an orange juice stand and bought a huge glassful for the equivalent of two cents, American currency, and decided to drop into Mariano Mercado's office before I ate the major part of my breakfast at Sanborn's.

I strolled down the Calle de Madellin until I reached the edifice which housed both the living quarters and office of Mariano Mercado, *detective particular.*

I climbed the dark flight of stairs, rapped on a door panel and heard Mercado's voice, freighted with anxiety, say: *"Adelante."*

I entered a room which would have delighted Pasteur. There were probably fewer bacteria in Mercado's living room than in any hospital. The chairs were of wood and leather, well-scrubbed each morning. No curtains concealed the windows. His desktop was bare save for an imposing array of bottles which stood like a battalion of soldiers ready to repel the first germ which approached Mariano Mercado.

There was no fabric in the room whatever. Cloth was a natural habitat for the invisible enemy. The entire apartment was as sanitary as it was uncomfortable. Since I had become an aide to Mercado, my back held a perpetual ache from sitting upright in his non-upholstered furniture.

I put my raincoat on the back of a chair and regarded my employer curiously. Most of him was dressed as usual—a flaming

Mercado landed on Palacios' shoulders. One spider-like brown hand snatched at the wrist which held the .38 and a bullet went through the ceiling of the hut.

combination of a zoot-suit lad who has just hit the numbers and a sixteenth-century Aztec emperor.

His suit was a recklessly cut green number with a belt in the back and lapels as wide as elephants' ears. His shirt was a flaming pink and his tie looked as if it had been dipped in a particularly happy rainbow. He was wearing one cerise sock and bright tan shoe. His left foot was bare.

As a matter of fact, his left foot was in his lap as he sat in the straight-backed chair before his desk. He was looking

at it like Eisenhower studying a map. His little black eyes were shrouded with worry and his brow was wrinkled in concentration.

"WELL," I said, "what's wrong?"

He lifted his head and faced me. He wore the Job-like expression of a man who is sorely tried but will not lose his patience.

"Dios mío," he said. "Why is it that I, who am so careful, must be constantly pursued by disease? Look at this!"

He waved his foot at me like a flag. I came closer and looked. I saw nothing and said so.

"*Cabrón!*" said Mariano Mercado. "Are you blind? Beyond all doubt I shall lose my second toe."

I peered at his second toe. At its base I perceived a tiny red mark. It could have been an insect bite or a pin prick. In any event it was something that the maddest hypochondriac never would have noticed.

"A mosquito," I said. "Or a scratch from your shoe."

"Mosquito!" shrieked Mercado. "Shoe! You are mad. It is ainhum."

"Ainhum?" I repeated, believing it to be a Spanish word which, like a number of others, was not contained in my vocabulary. "What is that in English?"

"*Hijo de perra!*" he howled. "It *is* English. Don't you know your own language?"

I did, of course. But I didn't know it as well as Mariano Mercado. Nor, for that matter, did any other American in Mexico.

"There are fifty-three diseases and disorders of the human foot," he said more quietly. "Ainhum will positively cause the loss of my second toe unless I can think of how to defeat the miserable germ which causes it."

Once more he went into a brown study. I shrugged, crossed the room to a bookshelf which contained nothing save various tomes on medicine. I selected a dictionary in English. I thumbed through until I came to ainhum.

I chuckled as I read. I put down the medical dictionary to find him glaring at me indignantly.

"You laugh at my losing a toe?"

"If you're losing anything, you're losing your mind. Now, look here, are you a Negro?"

He shook his head emphatically. "The blood of Castile flows in my veins."

"O.K. One more question. Since the mean temperature in this town is about seventy-six degrees Fahrenheit, you wouldn't call it the tropics, would you?"

"Of course not."

"And it's your second toe which is attacked, isn't it?"

"It is."

"Then relax. The book says that ainhum, in ninety-nine per cent of all cases attacks only Negroes in tropical countries. Moreover, it states that in one hundred per cent of all cases it attacks the little toe only. You're Castilian, you say. You don't live in the tropics, and it's your second toe which bothers you. Forget it."

"Forget it," he repeated bitterly. "What about the one per cent which is left over? That could be I, couldn't it?"

"What about the hundred per cent on the little toe angle?"

"The doctors have been wrong before, haven't they? They can be wrong now. I shall lose my second toe."

His little brown hand reached out and snatched up a bottle. He poured liquid lavishly on his foot. I sighed and picked up my raincoat.

"O.K.," I said. "Have a good time. I'm going over to Sanborn's for breakfast. I'll be back later."

"You'd better eat here," he said dolefully. "Do you know how many germs are on the cleanest restaurant plate?"

"Millions," I said hastily. I had heard this speech before. It went on for some time and I was hungry. My hand was on the door knob when a knock came at the panel and a moment later Coronel Breseda stepped into the room.

THE CORONEL was a member of *la policía*, an organization whose relations with Mercado were not of the most cordial. It was not that they sneered at him. On the contrary, they respected his brains and ability. But too often had he shown them up, too often had he stirred the sleeping dogs which the local police, for political and other reasons, preferred to let lie.

For this reason, *la policía* had put many obstacles in the germ-free path of Mariano Mercado. He was handed a summons on the slightest provocation. In Mexico where the little matter of obtaining a gun permit is more honored in the breach than in the observance, Mercado had lost his and was constantly being officiously searched for a gun he had no official right to carry.

Rather to my surprise, then, the coronel did not frown and slap a summons on Mercado's sterilized desk. Instead, he smiled beneath his swarthy mustachios and said with all the good will in the world: *"Buenos días, señor."*

Mercado looked up from his foot and nodded. I, being too hungry even to be curious as to the reason for this visit, muttered, *"Adíos,"* and went out for my breakfast.

In Sanborn's I was lucky to get a table. The place, as usual, was packed with American tourists. I ordered my breakfast, opened my paper and began to ingest the news. I heard the chair opposite me scrape back on the floor and a feminine voice say: "You don't mind if I sit here? There are no free tables just now."

With a grimace of annoyance I put my paper aside. As my gaze met the eyes of my companion my annoyance gave way to stark astonishment. Seated opposite me was a blonde, young and beyond all doubt beautiful.

That in itself may not appear odd. There are millions of blondes in the world, millions of beauties and many millions of young women.

But not, emphatically, Americans in Sanborn's in Mexico City.

In female tourists south of the border, the incidence of the grizzled, the garrulous, the ancient and the repulsive is too high, too consistent to be ascribed to luck. Doubtless it is the result of some hitherto undiscovered natural law. In four years I had never met a good-looking young blonde in Sanborn's. Now, I found myself gazing into the limpid blue eyes of one less than two feet away.

She threw a dazzling smile at me and said: "Do the waitresses speak English here?"

Most of them did but I was aware of a natural exhibitionistic desire. "Don't worry," I said. "Tell me what you want and I'll do it in Spanish."

She was touchingly grateful. By the time the eggs arrived she told me her name, which was Elsie Temple. Then, as I lingered over my coffee, masterminding the subtlest way of making a date for later, she did it for me.

"You know," she said, "I'm only a rather stupid tourist. You'll think I'm silly but somehow I don't trust the professional guides. What do you think?"

Well, as a matter of fact, the professional guide, licensed by the Mexican Government, is as trustworthy and courteous a character as you'll find in a day's ride. However, I hardly thought it polite to say so.

"For one as lovely as you," I said, "a guide would be most dangerous. Look here, why not let me show you the town?"

Her immediate gratitude, her immediate acceptance should have made me suspicious. But it didn't. A guy who has just won a bet at a hundred-to-one doesn't examine the bills to see if they're counterfeit.

"Suppose you pick me up at my hotel in an hour?" she said. "I have to go to a hairdresser first."

She stood up and so did I. As she was about to go, she said, as if she'd just thought of it: "I may be a little late.

You can't tell about these hairdressers. Suppose I give you my key. Then you won't have to wait with those awful people in the lobby. Go right up to my room."

She pressed a key into my hand and her high heels clattered over Sanborn's tiled floor. I stood staring after her in amazement. This sort of thing didn't happen—to me, at any rate.

I paid my check and hers and walked, in something of a daze, out into the sunlit street. I glanced up at the sky. A black cloud was riding in from the direction of Xochimilco. I estimated that the rain would begin in something under a half hour.

I spent fifteen minutes in a *cantina,* pouring a couple of quick ones down my gullet, then decided to wait for Elsie Temple in her hotel room.

CHAPTER TWO

TRUNKFUL OF MURDER

THE FARTHEST item from my mind as I unlocked the door in the hotel was Mariano Mercado. However, in thirty seconds he was my principal thought. The room, to my surprise, was empty.

I don't mean because Elsie Temple wasn't in it. I hadn't expected her to have arrived yet But there was nothing on the bureau and no bags or suitcases in sight. I stuck my head through the bathroom door, and outside of a fresh bar of hotel soap and a few unused towels there wasn't anything in there either. I went back into the bedroom, looked around at its bareness, then opened the closet.

Standing on its end was a huge tin trunk, with a label on it. I stared at it for a moment and reflected that it was odd that a woman as immaculately made up as Elsie

Temple hadn't unpacked a single thing since she had arrived in Mexico. I bent my head down, peered at the label, then gasped.

It was addressed to Mariano Mercado, *detective particular.*

I went over to the bed and sat down. I lighted a cigarette and gave myself over to thought. Had Elsie Temple merely shilled me into buying her breakfast in order to get me up here in her room to deliver a trunk to Mercado?

The thought was not only puzzling but most unpleasant to my ego. I looked at my watch. She was due in about twenty minutes. In my heart I did not believe she would come to this empty room. But with unreasonable hope, I waited.

I waited for half an hour. I picked up the phone, got the desk and asked for two porters. Heaven knows I didn't understand it, but two things were clear enough. First, the trunk was addressed to Mariano Mercado, hence it could be lawfully delivered to him. Second, I was confident that he could figure it all out more accurately than I could.

"Oh," said the porter in the doorway, "you are the *señor* who is to take the trunk?"

I flushed with anger and humiliation. Apparently, Elsie Temple had left word of my arrival even before she had set out for Sanborn's.

"*Sí,*" I said. "Take it downstairs and see if you can get it in a taxi."

The taxi, the trunk and I pulled up at Mercado's house some fifteen minutes later. A *cargador* lounged in the street, the ropes which were his badge of office, hanging about his neck. I showed him the trunk, gave him a peso and told him where to bring it. Then I went upstairs.

The first two items I became conscious of were that Mercado was now wearing his left shoe and the *coronel de policía* was still very much in evidence. Mercado was wearing such a self-satisfied smile I was certain he had overcome the sinister hosts that carried ainhum in their wake. The *coronel* did not appear so happy.

"You realize," he said, with the weary air of a man who has said the same thing several times before, "it is quite improper for me to come here. Quite humiliating. Yet for the cause of justice, I do it."

Mercado grinned. "Justice?" he said sweetly. "Are you certain the American ambassador isn't raising hell with the Foreign Office, which, in turn, is raising hell with you?"

The *coronel* didn't answer. I took advantage of the silence to say: "I have something for you. It's coming up. It's a—"

Mercado waved me to silence. "Please," he said. "*El Coronel* and I are having a most confidential conversation. It seems an American gentleman is missing."

"Missing?" I said. "Since when?"

"Since four o'clock this morning."

I looked at my watch. "And it's now ten-thirty. Have you guys gone naive or something? Thousands of tourists disappear for longer than that. You'll invariably find them in a *cantina*. What's all the excitement about?"

"This gentleman," said the *coronel* gravely, "is not in a *cantina*."

"If he is," said Mercado, "he's not enjoying himself. You see, Latham, the missing American is a corpse."

MY BEWILDERMENT evidently showed in my face. Mercado explained gently.

"His body was stolen from the undertaking establishment of Rayosso at four o'clock this morning. The American ambassador is annoyed. The *jefe de policía* is annoyed. The *gobernación* is annoyed. The coronel, here, seems to bear the brunt of their annoyances."

El Coronel leaned forward in his chair. "Now, look," he said, "will you help me or not? I guarantee restoration of your pistol permit. Moreover, I will let bygones be bygones. From now on you may depend upon the cooperation of the police."

Mariano Mercado gestured deprecatingly with his slim hands. As he spoke, the arrogance in his tone belied his words.

"And how can I help you? I, a humble *detective particular*, without the mighty resources of the police?"

El Coronel made a clucking, irritated sound with his tongue.

"Bien," he said. "You want me to admit you are intelligent. I do. Moreover, you know the confusing English language better than the Americans themselves. Besides, you have friends—underworld friends, who trust you. Now, will you help me find the corpse of Señor Albert Weldon?"

Mariano Mercado bowed gravely. "I accept. I shall deliver the corpse to you."

"When?"

Mercado held up his hand for silence. Outside in the corridor I heard the *cargador* lumbering along with his burden. I got up and opened the door for him. He brought the trunk in on his back and set it down in the middle of the room.

"Now," said Mariano Mercado.

"Now what?" I asked.

"El Coronel asked when I would deliver the body of Albert Weldon. I answered 'now.'"

"You mean the corpse is in this trunk? You expect us to find this Weldon guy in there?"

"As a matter of fact, I do," said Mercado. "Open it up. And remember, Coronel, the money in there belongs to me."

The colonel blinked and I gaped at him. Not only was he sure that the trunk contained a dead man but he seemed sure there was some cash in it as well.

I pushed the trunk over on its side, unbuckled its straps and fumbled with its brass catches. I flung open the lid.

There was a man inside—a dead man dressed respectably in a black suit. He was about sixty-odd years of age and even in death retained a distinguished expression on his pallid face. Behind me I heard *El Coronel* mutter: *"¡Válgame Dios!"* and then I saw the envelope pinned on to the lapel of the dead man's jacket.

It was addressed to Mariano Mercado. I detached it and handed it to him. He shuddered and pulled open the top drawer of his desk. He withdrew a pair of rubber gloves.

"Good heavens," he said, "you don't think that merely because a man is dead all the germs on him die, too, do you? Bacteria are breeding on that corpse like rabbits."

Not until he had carefully pulled on the gloves did he accept the envelope. He ripped it open. I saw the green flash of a few five-hundred-peso notes and he thrust them hurriedly into his pocket. Then he showed us the sheet of notepaper in which the money had been wrapped. It read:

Sr. Mercado:

Here is a fee for you. Please find out who killed me. First, I suggest a post-mortem.

Albert Weldon

"*Dios,*" murmured the colonel. "And how did you know this trunk was coming, *señor?* How—"

Mercado waved a deprecating hand. "I have my sources," he said. "Now, will you kindly remove the body. It is most unsanitary to have it lying around in this climate. Do you realize what infection could result in only—"

"*Sí, sí,*" said *El Coronel* hastily, indicating that he had heard Mercado's health speeches before. "I shall have it removed at once."

"And the post-mortem?" asked Mercado. "Certainly, under the circumstances, you must arrange for that."

"Indeed, *amigo.* I shall inform you of the result immediately. I am most grateful for your cooperation."

"*Por nada,*" said Mercado. "But for God's sake get it out of here right away."

In Mexico, the authorities do not stand on such formality as in the United States. *El Coronel* bothered with no documents nor did he waste time in calling an ambulance or hearse. He simply went down into the street, hired another *cargador* who bore the Grand Rapids coffin off on his straining back.

WHEN THEY had left, Mercado and I eyed each other suspiciously. He removed his rubber gloves and said: "And how did you know that trunk was coming up, my friend?"

"You're asking me? How did you know? Moreover, how did you know there was a corpse inside it?"

His little black eyes bored into mine and I cracked first. "All right," I said. "I met a beautiful tourist in Sanborn's. I—"

He grinned. "A beautiful tourist in Sanborn's? I hope the rest of your story is more credible than that."

"As a matter of fact, it isn't. This is what happened."

I told him of my meeting with Elsie Temple, of my visiting her hotel room and finding the trunk addressed to Mercado. When I finished he pursed up his lips and regarded the far wall thoughtfully.

"All right," I said, "I've told you my end of it. How did you know the trunk was coming?"

"Someone phoned me while *El Coronel* was here. It was a woman. Probably this Temple girl. She pleaded with me to investigate the case. Told me a body was on the way up here with fee attached. She insisted a post-mortem would prove murder, not suicide."

"Was Weldon supposed to have killed himself? What's it all about?"

Behind him, the window shade fluttered in the warm breeze. Mariano Mercado shuddered, got up and closed the window. The outside temperature was at the moment exactly seventy-four degrees.

"A draft," he said, "is a lethal thing. Do you know what happens to the body when it is exposed to a—"

"Sure," I said hurriedly. "It gets cold and weak and all the germs in Christendom enter and kill you. But what about Albert Weldon?"

Mercado gazed at me reproachfully, sighed, and to my relief dropped the subject of drafts.

"Weldon was a wealthy American. Sometimes, Latham, I wonder are there any other kind?"

"Millions," I told him. "But they don't have the carfare to come down here on their vacations. But go on."

"Well, Weldon has been in Mexico City for some three months. I'm not sure why he came. The *policía* seem to believe he was here for the purpose of snapping up one of our easy divorces. During his first week in our country he was in an automobile accident. He wasn't badly injured but he was scared to death. He developed a nervous breakdown. He's been under a doctor's care for over two months."

"Did he come down alone?"

Mercado coughed, looked worried and snatched a bottle from the gleaming array on his desk. With an expression of grave concern, he sniffed a couple of nose drops.

"No," he said at last, "he did not come down alone. He brought with him his son, his niece who is an orphan and has lived with him for years, and a secretary. They all testify that Weldon, since his accident, suffered from acute melancholia."

"It sounds easy enough so far," I said. "How did he kill himself—always provided he *did* kill himself?"

"Sleeping tablets with a high content of barbitol. He usually took one or two each night. The evening he died, he apparently took the whole damned bottle. It was found empty at his bedside."

I nodded. "So, I take it, the doctors said suicide and they bundled him off to Rayosso's for shipment back to the States. They planned no post-mortem?"

"As you know," said Mercado, "we're not too fussy about those things down here. It looked like an open-and-shut case of suicide and the ambassador thought Weldon's family would object to us cutting him up to find out for certain if it really was sleeping tablets which killed him. It seemed obvious enough that they did."

I LIGHTED a cigarette as Mercado watched me disapprovingly. Before he could deliver a monologue on the evils of tobacco, I said: "And someone, probably this Temple dame, thinks Weldon was murdered. So she, and doubtless some confederates, swiped the corpse, sent it along to you, along with a few hundred pesos to get it post-mortemed. And I was the fall guy!" I thought it over for a moment. "It was a damned roundabout way of doing it."

"That's what puzzles me. If this girl-friend of yours had something, why didn't she give it to the authorities? She can go to jail for five years for swiping that body."

"How the devil *did* she swipe it?"

"She apparently didn't. Two men, Mexicans, probably hired by her, tied up the watchman and walked out with the coffin which they loaded on a truck."

I stood up and shrugged my shoulders. "Well," I said, "it's a cinch this Temple woman isn't going through all these shenanigans just for the hell of it. I suppose the old guy was murdered at that. Someone probably stuck a poisoned pill in the bottle of sleeping tablets. Then when the old guy took it, the murderer emptied the rest of the pills down the can to make it look as if Weldon knocked them all off, thus committing suicide."

Mercado made a palm-spreading gesture. "Perhaps," he said. "But why speculate when it isn't necessary? *El Coronel's* report will answer our questions."

I picked up a copy of the morning *Universal* and studied the entries of the *Hipodromo*. Mercado removed his shoe again and applied a liberal dose of antiseptic to the ainhum he didn't have. We engaged in these respective pursuits for the better part of two hours. Then the telephone rang.

Despite the fact that he was a damned sight closer to it than I was, Mercado glanced significantly at me. Answering the phone was one of my more important duties. According to him, the legion of bacteria that lay ambushed in a telephone mouthpiece shouldn't even happen in Hitler's drinking glass.

I picked it up, said, *"Bueno,"* and listened to *El Coronel's* rapid Spanish. After I got him to slow up a bit, I understood the words he was saying, but that was all I understood.

I hung up, puzzled. Mercado said: "Well, what does he say?"

"Indirectly, that Elsie Temple is a nut."

"And directly?"

"That Weldon was a suicide. His tummy is full of barbitol. Apparently, he took about fifteen or twenty tablets."

Mariano Mercado grunted and bit his lip. His brown brow wore a frown. A fly that had somehow avoided the screens on the window buzzed into the room. Mercado seized a Flit sprayer like Patton taking Brest. I waited patiently. I knew he would deliver no opinion in the matter of Albert Weldon until the insect had been vanquished.

He got it on the third blast and resumed his seat. I figured I'd better say something before he delivered a very familiar speech on the house fly as a carrier of disease.

"So it must have been suicide, after all, eh? You can't very well pour a bottle of pills down a guy's gullet, can you?"

"Maybe, Latham, you can. Anyway, this Temple girl was certain enough of foul play to send me two thousand pesos. The least we can do is look into the matter."

He stood up, went to the closet and took out a topcoat. It was the color of light chocolate and its buttons were wonderful discs of nacre. I shuddered as I looked at it. He carefully wrapped a yellow woolen scarf about his thin neck, pulled on a pair of gloves, and said: "Come on."

"Where?"

"To Weldon's hotel. Let us talk to his family. We may pick up something."

I glanced at him. "You're forgetting something, aren't you?"

"What?"

"It's the rainy season, you know."

"Dios mío, I forgot," he said fervently. "Latham, you may have saved my life."

I watched him, grinning, as he returned to the closet. He hooked an umbrella over one arm and slung a raincoat over the other. Now he was ready to venture into the bright Mexican sunlight.

CHAPTER THREE
SWAMI SLAY

WE TOOK a taxi to the De Soto Hotel where Weldon had rented a suite. Mercado, by dint of some judicious lies concerning his official position, obtained entrance. We were led into a vast Spanish drawing room by a servant. Mercado announced to the two men and the girl in the room that we were confidential operatives of *la policía.*

Ronald Weldon, the dead man's son, was a tall blond man of about thirty-two. He was well-dressed and his gray eyes made him appear forthright and frank. He introduced us first to his cousin, Mary Hutton. She was a dark girl, with deep smoldering eyes, of medium height and a build that would have made her most popular in a foxhole.

Washburn, Weldon's secretary, was a bald, fussy little man, with rimless glasses and an air of intense activity. Ronald offered us chairs and Washburn hustled to the phone to order us drinks from the bar.

"The police telephoned us a little while ago," said young Weldon. "Naturally, we are happy that my father's body has been recovered. But we can't understand why it was stolen. It just doesn't make any sense."

A *mesero* came in with a tray of drinks. Mercado most impolitely wiped the rim of his glass with his handkerchief before he imbibed. Then he sighed and said gently: "Do you mind if I ask a few rather personal questions?"

"Questions?" said Washburn, annoyance in his tone. "My God, we have enough tragedy here. Why more questions? Since Mr. Weldon's body has been recovered, let's ship it home and forget about it. It seems quite unnecessary—"

Mary Hutton waved him to silence. "If you think your questions can throw any light on this weird business, by all means ask them. Am I right, Ronald?"

"Of course," said Ronald Weldon. "Ask away, Señor Mercado."

Mercado cleared his throat. "First," he said, "who benefits under Mr. Weldon's will?"

"We all do," said Ronald Weldon simply. "My mother is dead. My cousin Mary, here, and myself split most of the estate. Mr. Washburn gets a handsome bequest."

Washburn's face turned slowly red. "Sir," he said angrily, "you are not inferring that—"

Mercado shook his head sadly. The unfamiliarity of Americans with their own language invariably pained him. "The speaker implies," he said. "The hearer infers. But let's get on with it. Which of you found Mr. Weldon's body?"

"I did," said Ronald. "He was dead when I went in to awaken him for breakfast. The bottle of sleeping tablets on the table by the bed was empty."

"Where did you buy these tablets?"

"At the drugstore on the corner. Guerrero's, I think the name is. Why?"

Mercado looked slowly around the room. "Now," he said, "do any of you know a young woman named Elsie Temple?"

My gaze followed his, searching for any telltale expression on any of the three faces. I saw nothing. The three heads shook slowly.

"No," said Ronald. "Never heard of her. Who is she?"

Mariano Mercado didn't answer. He stood up and walked around the room, frowning heavily.

"Estoy preocupado," he muttered.

"Why should you be worried? Or even concerned?" snapped Washburn, who obviously understood Spanish. "Mr. Weldon is by now back at Rayosso's. He will be sent back home and interred properly. The episode of the kidnaping of the corpse is best forgotten. Though I should think you'd find the culprits and punish them."

Mary Hutton nodded agreement. "Of course," she said, "it is mysterious, but since Uncle has been found, unimportant. There is no need for you to concern yourself about it, *señor.*"

"But I do concern myself about it," said Mercado. "I am a detective. Naturally, I concern myself with mysterious occurrences. You might as well ask a general not to concern himself with the war."

"Well," said Mary Hutton smiling faintly, "the generals won't have to concern themselves with the war either, after December ninth."

She spoke with an air of quiet authority. We all turned and looked at her.

"How can you say that, Mary?" asked Ronald, bewildered.

She shrugged. "I guess I should have kept my mouth shut, but you'll see that I am right."

Mercado fixed her with his polished black button eyes. "So, *señorita*, you actually know the date of the war's end?"

The girl again shrugged shapely shoulders. "What's the difference? I told you I should have kept my mouth shut. None of you will believe me."

"May I ask," pressed Mercado, "how you happen to know this?"

"I was told."

"By whom?"

There was a long silence. For a while, I thought she would not answer. Then she said, with an odd smile: "Not that it will mean anything to you, but it was a man, an Irishman named Doyle. A.C. Doyle."

Mercado drew a deep breath. Then he took up his umbrella and raincoat, heaped profuse Latin thank-you's upon the assembly and headed for the door. I trailed along behind.

I STILL trailed along as we gained the street and Mercado strode into the corner *cantina*. He ordered *habanero*. So did I. I emptied my glass while he was still fussing around wiping the bacteria from the rim of his. I said: "Well, did we find out anything?"

"I'm not sure," he answered glumly.

He sighed heavily and drained his *habanero*. Idly, he picked up a newspaper lying on the bar. His eye ran down the advertisements on the amusement page. His gaze paused on an twelve-inch display.

"My God!" he said. "Colimo!"

I read the ad over his shoulder, although I didn't have to. Everyone in Mexico knew about Colimo.

"Come on," he said. "Quickly."

He trotted from the *cantina* with me at his heels. We clambered into a taxi. He said to the driver: "*Avenida Hamburgo. La casa del Señor Colimo. Rápidamente!*"

I blinked at him. "Colimo's?" I said. "What are we going to do? Psychic research?"

He blinked lazily in the sunlight which poured through the window which he had cautiously closed. He remained silent. I shrugged my shoulders and tried to figure it.

Colimo had been front-page news lately. He was, in my opinion and that of the American Institute of Psychical Research, a charlatan. However, to others he was a man of miracles, the greatest spiritualistic medium the world had ever seen.

Of late, he had submitted to various tests made by eminent skeptics. While he had failed to convince them, they certainly had also failed to prove that Colimo was a fraud. The papers on both sides of the border had been filled with his exploits, and his take from superstitious Mexicans and American tourist trade was reported, probably quite accurately, to be terrific.

We clambered out of the cab before a neat white house some few blocks from the American Embassy. This time, Mercado paid the driver. We marched on to the porch. I rang the doorbell.

I stood there for a long moment and lighted a cigarette as I waited. Mercado coughed silently and his brow screwed up in hypochondriac anxiety. Then, from within the house, came two staccato, familiar sounds. I glanced apprehensively at Mercado.

"Shots?"

He nodded. "Better try your shoulder on the door."

I drew a deep breath, tensed and moved forward. As I did so, the door flew suddenly outward. The panel smacked me squarely in the face and I found myself deposited on the lawn. A feminine voice, which even at that moment, sounded as if I had heard it somewhere before, shrieked: "He's dead! He's been murdered. For God's sake—"

Mercado dashed into the house, his little brown hand tugging at the revolver in his hip pocket. I took my nose out of a flower bed and looked around. Just beyond the gate a woman was getting into a waiting taxi I had not noticed before. As the cab pulled away I got a single flash of her white, scared face. It was, beyond all doubt, Elsie Temple.

I swore beneath my breath, clambered to my feet and ran out to the street. The cab had already rounded the corner. I swore again. I heard another shot from inside the house. I raced up the garden path into the carpeted hall.

To my left was an open door. I entered a heavily-curtained room, and incense poured into my nostrils. At the rear was another door, open and leading into a kitchen.

Mercado sat on the windowsill, his revolver in his hand. He squinted along its barrel and fired again. Then he sighed and said: "Too late. An instant too late."

"For what?" I panted.

"Either to prevent the murder or catch the murderer."

"Good Lord, who's murdered? Where's the murderer?"

"The murderer has just ridden toward the Paseo de Reforma on a motorcycle he had parked out in the back alley there. The corpse is Colimo. Didn't you see him?"

I shook my head. Mercado walked back into the other room, beckoned me to follow him.

IN THE darkened living room, Colimo was seated in an ebony chair, his head slumped on an ebony table. The black wood ran red with blood and there were two holes in Colimo's head.

I blinked, lit another cigarette and stared at Mercado in awed wonder.

"Heavens!" I said. "Is this why you came here? You knew Colimo was going to be killed?"

He shook his head. "I had no idea," he said. "I came here for information. Let's see if we can get it before the police arrive. That woman who ran screaming from here will doubtless inform them."

I remembered then. I told him excitedly that I had recognized the fleeing woman as Elsie Temple. His brow wrinkled in thought. He coughed again and said, a note of alarm in his voice: "Latham, open the windows. That damned incense probably weakens the lungs."

I pulled back the heavy curtains and flung open the wide windows. The sunlight streamed into the room. Mercado paced back and forth across the thick carpet. He halted suddenly before a black, vast desk. He picked up a check, grunted.

"On *El Banco Nacional*. Drawn to Colimo for two hundred pesos. Signed by Elsie Thackeray. What did you say that woman told you her name was?"

"Elsie Temple," I said. "But I bet it's the same woman. Naturally, she'd give me a phony name."

"Good. We should be able to get a line on her from the bank."

He opened a leather ledger on the desk. "His appointment book," he muttered. He thumbed through its pages, snapped it shut and grinned. "I rather thought so," he said. "Now, let's see if there is anything else."

He proceeded to frisk the place thoroughly. From his lack of enthusiasm as he finished, I gathered there was nothing else. A few minutes later, a big black car drove up to the house. Three men came up to the open door. They were all in uniform and one of them was *El Coronel*.

El Coronel gazed at Mercado with suspicion.

"Wherever there is a corpse," he said, "I find you. I do not like it. I suspect you know more of this than I do."

"A natural suspicion," said Mariano Mercado.

El Coronel bit his lip as his men examined the corpse of Colimo. "Today, I returned to you your pistol permit because I asked your aid in recovering a body. Even as I spoke to you, you apparently knew it was on the way to your office. You tricked me. Now, I find you here with an entirely different corpse. I do not like it."

He held out his hand, palm upward. "Your gun, please."

Mercado sighed sadly. "You mean it's been revoked again."

"Again."

Slowly, Mercado took his heavy .45 from his pocket and handed it over.

"Now," said *El Coronel*, "what are you doing here, may I ask?"

"Discharging a duty to a client. Investigating the murder of Albert Weldon."

"*Cabrón!* Weldon was a suicide. The postmortem proved that positively. And what has Colimo's death to do with it?"

"I shall inform you at the time of the arrest. In the meantime, I should like to make a request."

"What?"

"Do you have the bottle that contained the pills which apparently killed Weldon?"

"Naturally. What of it?"

"I should like to have it."

"Why?"

"I need it in my investigations."

EL CORONEL hesitated. He had little affection for Mercado. But there had been times when Mercado had been very, very right. Mercado pressed his opportunity.

"I give you my word," he said, "that should I develop anything in the case, I shall inform you first. The arrest shall be yours."

El Coronel screwed up his brow and considered. "Very well," he said. "You may have the bottle. However, you may not have the revolver. Moreover, what are you two doing at the scene of a murder?"

"Colimo was dead when we entered," said Mercado. "The woman who doubtless called you is the witness you want. Latham and I can bear each other out. Colimo was dead when we arrived."

El Coronel reluctantly accepted this.

"You," said. Mercado to me, "accompany *El Coronel* to the police headquarters and obtain the bottle. I must go to the *Banco Nacional*."

He strode out of the house, his brow creased in thought. *El Coronel* gazed after him, frank annoyance stamped on his swarthy features.

Some ninety minutes later, I returned to Mercado's sterile apartment to find him sitting at his desk. I laid the wrapped-up pill bottle before him.

"Now," I said, "where are we?"

"In a very interesting position," he said. "I called at the bank upon which that Thackeray woman's check was drawn. I am now certain she is the same person as this Temple who played you for such a sucker."

"That's rather obvious," I told him. "Is that all?"

He shook his head. "The bank told me that when she opened the account she asked them to recommend a lawyer. They gave me his name. I visited him.

"A most enlightening result. Mrs. Thackeray came down here to obtain a divorce from her husband back in the States."

"What's enlightening about that?"

He looked at me, shook his head sadly as if mourning my lost wits. Then, he picked up the bottle and removed its outer covering of tissue paper.

He read aloud the name of the druggist on the label. Then he grunted and stared intently at the scribbled writing on it. He ran his thumb slowly back and forth over the sticker. He muttered, *"Pues, pues,"* over and over to himself. He finally lifted his head and caught my eye.

"Latham, go to this drugstore. Take the bottle with you. Ask them how many prescriptions of these pills they made up for Weldon. Ask them if they made up any other prescriptions. If so, find out what they were."

"All right," I said. "But I hope you know what we're doing. I don't."

CHAPTER FOUR

QUERETARO QUARRY

I GOT back in a half hour with my report. "This is the only stuff they ever prepared for Weldon," I told him.

"Three times they filled this bottle. The only difference was that the last time the capsules were different."

"The capsules were different? What does that mean?"

"The little translucent containers the powders are packed in. You've seen them often enough. Sometimes, they're white, sometimes yellow, sometimes pink or red."

"And what about these?"

"Well, in the first two bottles white capsules were used to hold the powders. In the last prescription, the druggist used pink, since he had a lot of them lying around."

Mariano Mercado cleared his throat, picked up an atomizer and sprayed his larynx at great length. He replaced it among the array of bottles on his desk and said: "This is most interesting, Latham. Let us suppose that one of Señor Weldon's menage hired a killer to murder Colimo. It seems logical that the principal would not pay the assassin in advance, *no es verdad?*"

"Granting your original assumption, no. But why assume one of Weldon's menage hired an assassin for any such purpose as killing Colimo?"

He did not answer that. He continued as if I had not spoken.

"Moreover, it is unlikely that the killer would go to the hotel to collect his fee. Hence, he will probably phone, either arranging a rendezvous, or give a mailing address."

He slapped his hands together decisively. "Latham, go to the Weldon's hotel. The phone operator doubtless speaks English. Bribe her."

I was completely bewildered by this time. "Bribe her to do what?"

"To inform us if and when someone calls the Weldon suite—a Mexican, mark you, not an American—and either makes an appointment to meet someone or leaves a post-office address."

I stood up and sighed. "I don't know what the devil you're doing," I told him. "But suppose this mythical caller doesn't call but writes?"

"On that we must gamble. If that happens we must use different and more difficult methods. It will all be much easier if he telephones. "

I shrugged my shoulders, went downstairs and took a taxi to the hotel.

The telephone operator was a good-looking girl who spoke English quite well. It cost me two hundred pesos.

The following afternoon he got the call. He hung up the receiver, and, for one of the few times since I had known him, evinced some slight excitement about something other than bacteria.

"The call came in," he announced. "Long distance from Queretaro. Some *hombre* gave the name of Palacios and *listo* address."

Listo was general delivery and Queretaro was a hundred-odd miles north. "So what do we do now?"

"Go there. Bring the car around. We've got to get there before the letter."

"Do I gather that you expect we'll pick up the guy you saw escape from Colimo's and nab him in the act of collecting for his killing?"

"Exactly. Get the car."

WE ARRIVED at Queretaro a little after three in the afternoon. Mercado had given me a detailed description of the man he had seen escaping from Colimo's swami parlor. We took up our positions discreetly at the far end of the post-office and kept our eyes glued to the general delivery window.

Precisely what Mercado was up to, I didn't know. This *hombre* Palacios was doubtless guilty of the murder of Colimo, but how that tied up with Weldon or my little blond pal who had swiped Weldon's corpse from the undertaking establishment was utterly beyond me.

We had kept the vigil for some two hours. Closing time was approaching and I wasn't upset about that. This was a dull job. I far preferred the congeniality of the hotel *cantina*. Then Mercado, a fanatic on the subject of regularity, had to visit the men's room.

That left me on my own for some ten minutes. And, as I might have known, with my luck, that was when Palacios put in his appearance.

At first I wasn't sure, as I saw the stocky, swarthy man approach the grilled window. Verbal descriptions can be tricky and, as a foreigner, I didn't want to make a mistake and put the arm on some solid local citizen.

I watched him intently as he went to the window and received a large envelope. Then he went out into the street, while I stood praying that Mercado would put in a hasty reappearance.

The stocky man hailed a taxi. I moved forward, then stopped abruptly, wondering what the hell I was supposed to do even if I were certain of his identity.

I was unarmed and if he were the killer he certainly was not. Moreover, my accent gave me away as a foreigner, and if a brawl ensued, public sentiment, always feverish in Mexico, would be on the side of my adversary.

Even as I hesitated, Palacios climbed into the taxi and Mercado came running up to my side.

"That is he!" he cried. *"Dios,* you've let him get away."

He cursed under his breath and his lips moved as he memorized the license number of the taxi. Then he led the way into a *cantina*, berating me bitterly.

"My God!" I said. "What was I supposed to do? Close with him unarmed?"

"Why not?" said Mercado coldly. "I would have."

I knew he would have. The only thing he feared were the bacterial hosts. We drank several *habaneros*, then went about checking the taxicab.

It didn't prove difficult. We found the company which owned the hack easily enough and simply waited for the driver to come in. He was quite cooperative.

It seemed he had driven our quarry off the main highway some thirty miles north, along a dirt road to a cabin facing a ruined, uninhabited hacienda. Thirty minutes later, I was driving Mercado's car over the same route.

I got lost twice and it was after midnight when we finally saw the stark ruins of the old hacienda rising against the clouding sky. I halted the car a good hundred yards down the road. Then, as we approached, we saw the thatched hut on the side of the trail opposite the hacienda.

"What do we do now?" I asked.

"Approach noiselessly," said Mercado. "Come on."

Without any enthusiasm whatever, I followed him.

Evidently Palacios was sure of the inaccessibility of his hideout. The front door was unlocked. We entered a dark room and heard faint snoring.

"He's asleep," said Mercado. "He'll probably sleep all night. Go back to Queretaro. Phone *El Coronel*. Tell him to start for here immediately, and bring with him all the principals. Mary Hutton, Washburn, Ronald Weldon and that Thackeray woman. Incidentally, she's at the Ritz Hotel.

Her bank told me. Then wait for him. Pick him up in Queretaro and then come out here."

"And what are you going to do?"

"Wait. There's a bare possibility he may wake up and move out. Someone's got to stay here, to follow him if he moves anywhere. He probably won't, but we can't gamble."

"You can't wait here in the house," I protested. "If he gets up for any reason he'll find you. And he'll have a gun."

We thought this over for a silent moment.

"Look," I said, "if he intends to go away, he'll certainly come out the front door and set off down the road. You can plant yourself across the road, there. Hide in the hacienda and watch. That's safer."

"All right," he whispered. "But hurry. Get out to the car. Right away."

I went out into the muddy road again. As I did so the heavens split above me. There was a crash of thunder. The rain pelted down in sheets. I was drenched as I climbed into the car.

I set off, praying the thunder hadn't awakened Palacios before Mercado had got across to the hacienda.

IT WAS almost dawn when *El Coronel* picked me up in Queretaro. He had two cars with him, each driven by coppers, also the entire Weldon menage and Elsie Temple, or Thackeray.

I left Mercado's coupe parked at the curb and climbed in alongside *El Coronel* in order to direct the driver. In reply to his questioning, I could only tell him that I knew little more than he did.

It was still pelting rain, as it had been all night, when we started out to the thatched hut in the wilderness.

A Mexican policeman drives a car only slightly less recklessly than a World War I pilot engaging in a dog fight. We sped through the driving rain and I feared my ultimate fate more than Mariano Mercado feared leprosy.

Water pelted against the windshield, obscuring our vision. We skidded perilously a score of times. But neither of these circumstances had the smallest cautionary effect on our white-toothed, beaming driver. He was a copper with the right of way, and rain, snow or high water, he was taking every advantage of it.

We turned into the mired dirt road to the left and I was pleased to observe that, perforce, our speed decreased some ten kilometers an hour. I peered through the rear window. I saw the white, frightened faces of the two women in the car behind. I noted that their driver was beaming, happily and toothily, as well.

I sighed and wondered how Mercado was doing. I felt fairly certain that our killer would not precipitately abandon his hideaway. And for that I was grateful. I didn't relish a Wild West pursuit with my little brown Barney Oldfield at the wheel.

Dawn had come up now. The sky was gray and overcast, the color of a rather melancholy oyster. We raced wildly past pepper trees whose leaves dripped and an occasional thatched hut with a patient and drenched burro tethered outside.

Then, peering through the steamy windshield, I saw the cabin in the distance. Smoke curled dispiritedly from the thatch of its roof. I nudged *El Coronel* and drew his attention to it. Apparently, our man was preparing his breakfast. I glanced at the other side of the road up ahead, seeking some sign of Mercado in the ruins of the hacienda. I saw nothing, save the depressing pile of granite rising against the slate sky.

A hundred yards this side of the hut stood a thick clump of Indian laurels. *El Coronel* tapped the driver on the shoulder and muttered: *"Para aquí!"*

We emerged into the blinding rain. *El Coronel* signaled the copper in the other car to remain there with his customers. Our chauffeur, *El Coronel*, and I sloshed through the mud toward the cabin.

"I would prefer that the Americans remained out of the shooting, if any," said *El Coronel* by way of explanation.

As we gained the entrance of the hideout, I glanced again at the old hacienda, hoping that Mercado would put in an appearance at any minute. If he was still there, watching, he certainly must have seen us. However, I caught no sign of him.

El Coronel and the copper unbuttoned the flaps of their holsters. I discreetly took up my position behind them and we single-filed into the house. Through the arched opening which led from what was, I supposed, the living room, I saw our murderer bent over the charcoal stove preparing his breakfast. The smell of strong Mexican coffee assailed my nostrils and I found myself wishing I was sitting down to a stack of wheatcakes at Sanborn's.

El Coronel's boot thudded on the hard-packed earth floor. The killer swung about. As he did so, he snatched up a heavy .38 which must have been lying conveniently on the stove top at his side.

Neither *El Coronel* nor his aide, it appeared, were any rivals of Gene Autrey on the draw. Their hands had barely touched their revolver butts when the muzzle from the kitchen had them covered.

There was an instant's hesitation on everyone's part. I considered for a moment throwing myself, face first, into the yellow mud at the side of the road. Then, on the side of the kitchen behind our murderer and a foot to his left, a cupboard door opened. I watched it, fascinated.

Mariano Mercado's familiar face peered out. His collar was horribly wrinkled and his flamboyant tie awry. He blinked at us, inhaled sibilantly and sprang like a puma.

HE LANDED on our adversary's shoulders. One spider-like brown hand snatched at the wrist which held the .38. The pair went to the floor and a bullet went through the ceiling.

El Coronel snapped his fingers and his subordinate leaped into the fray. In another moment, the man beneath Mercado was disarmed. Both he and Mercado got to their feet. *El Coronel* stared at our quarry.

"So," he said, "Palacios, eh? At last you are delivered into the hands of the law."

Palacios shot something back in such rapid Spanish I could barely translate it. I gathered it was the Mexican equivalent of: "You ain't got anything on me, copper."

"You know this *hombre?*" asked Mercado.

El Coronel nodded. "Too damned well. We've never convicted him, though. I am certain, however, he is guilty of every crime on the statutes."

"Well," said Mercado, "you can have him for murder this time. Where are the people I told you to bring, Latham?"

"In another car. Down by the laurels."

"Get them."

El Coronel looked at him curiously. He nodded to the other copper who went clopping through the mud down to the parked cars. *El Coronel* held his gun on Palacios who glared at him defiantly. Mercado sighed. He straightened his tie and buttoned his coat. He looked sleepy and far less dapper than was his wont.

By now I had recovered somewhat. A thought came to me. "What the devil were you doing in that cupboard? My God, it's so tiny I don't see how you got in it at all."

"I stayed in the kitchen all night," he said. "Then when I heard Palacios getting up, I hid in the cupboard. I figured he'd want some breakfast."

"But why didn't you go across the road to the old hacienda? You could have spotted Palacios if he'd left the house. Are you loco, to stay here unarmed? Suppose he got up and found you? Suppose he'd looked in the cupboard? Suppose—"

I was interrupted by the arrival of the two chauffeur-coppers and the remainder of the caravan. We joined them in the living room. Elsie Thackeray looked as if she had been weeping. The Hutton girl was tired and pale, but self-possessed. Young Weldon bore himself as a man bewildered, but resolved to be patient until matters are explained to him, while Washburn was frankly and audibly annoyed.

"This is the most high-handed proceeding I have ever witnessed," he barked. "How dare you drag us out here? Well, answer me!"

He glared at *El Coronel,* who in turn regarded Mercado with a mixture of hope and annoyance.

"We are here," said Mercado gravely, "to clear up two murder cases. That of Señor Weldon and Colimo, the medium."

"Then do so," said young Weldon, "and let's get out of this godforsaken spot and back to town."

"Well," said Mercado, "the killer of Colimo is obvious. It's Palacios here. I saw him flee the scene of the killing and I am certain that Mrs. Thackeray, here, can identify him, too."

Elsie Thackeray nodded her head slowly. She appeared as if she were about to speak, then caught my eye and hastily averted her gaze.

"This is fantastic," sputtered Palacios in English a little more broken than my Spanish. "I shall beat you in the courts. I shall have the very high-priced lawyers."

"What will you hire them with?" asked *El Coronel*. "You never had more than five hundred pesos at one time in your life."

"I have now," said Palacios aloofly.

Mariano Mercado nodded. "Quite probably, he has."

"You mean," I said, "that he was paid to kill Colimo? That's where he got this dough?"

"You have it," said Mercado. "That's exactly what happened."

"This is all very well," snapped Washburn. "But what has it to do with the death of Mr. Weldon, who quite obviously committed suicide anyway?"

"Oh, no, he didn't," said Mercado.

El Coronel sighed. "Look," he said, "you concede the truth of the post-mortem? You admit that Señor Weldon died of an overdose of those sleeping tablets?"

"That I admit."

"Then, *válgame Dios*," said *El Coronel*, "you're not arguing that someone held him and forced those damned pills down his gullet? Someone in the suite would have heard the struggle."

"I contend no such thing," said Mercado. "I admit that Weldon took the pills of his own volition."

El Coronel shuddered. "Then what the devil are we all doing out here in the wilderness? One copper is all you needed to bring Palacios in for the murder of Colimo. Mrs. Thackeray could have identified him in town."

Mariano Mercado's sigh swept through the room like a dispirited breeze. "You don't understand," he said. "No one understands— save myself and the murderer."

"The murderer? You mean Palacios?"

"No," said Mercado slowly. "I do not mean Palacios."

CHAPTER FIVE

PINK AS IN POISON

BY THIS time he had all of us on edge. But I knew better than to hurry him. He was very stubborn at times like this.

"Look, *señor*," said Mary Hutton to *El Coronel*. "I assume we have been brought here for some purpose. Will you please tell the horribly-dressed little man to get on with it?"

Mercado blinked, then flushed. He regarded the girl with utter amazement. It was utterly inconceivable to him that anyone could consider his garb anything save the height of refined fashion. He shrugged his shoulders delicately, muttered something in Spanish about gringo barbarians, and let it go at that.

Then he groped in his pocket and produced the empty pill bottle which had been found at the side of Albert Weldon's bed.

"I don't know whether or not you investigated," he said to *El Coronel*, "but these powders are put up in capsule form. The capsules are of various colors. For instance, the first two bottles prepared for Señor Weldon contained the powder in white capsules, the last bottle, pink capsules."

"That's true," said Washburn. "I bought the last bottle myself. What of it?"

Mercado held up the bottle. "If you'll examine the label closely, you'll find that there is some gum, or mucilage, on the outside over the writing."

He paused and beamed around the room at all our uncomprehending faces. Then, he said, with the air of a man who has just made an incontestable point: "Now, let's get to the motive."

"What motive?" bellowed *El Coronel.*

"Why, the motive for the murder I have just explained to you."

I thought, for a moment, that *El Coronel* was going to bang him over the head with a pistol butt. However, with a visible and tremendous effort, he controlled himself.

"Have you just explained a murder?" he asked tensely.

"Of course. Now the motive. Mrs. Thackeray, why did you come to Mexico?"

Elsie Thackeray looked at him. Her lips moved feebly, but no words came.

"I shall answer for you," said Mercado. "You came for a speedy divorce, did you not? That much I know. Your bank told me they had recommended a lawyer at your request. Your lawyer told me why you retained him."

Mrs. Thackeray nodded again. "Yes," she said softly, "I came for a divorce."

"Good," said Mercado. "Now, do any of you know, outside of Mrs. Thackeray, why Weldon came to Mexico?"

There was a long silence in the room. "Very well," said Mercado. "I shall tell you that, too."

He paused for a moment, then continued. "Weldon came not for a divorce. On the contrary, he came for a marriage. He came to marry Mrs. Thackeray as soon as she had severed her own matrimonial ties."

"That's a lie!" This was young Weldon, and he seemed angry.

"It is no lie," said Mercado. "Ask Mrs. Thackeray. Now, naturally, if Señor Weldon had a wife, his estate would no longer be split two ways—between his son and his niece. So, you see, I have first explained the method of murder, now I make clear the motivation."

EL CORONEL suddenly lost his air of annoyance. His tone was professionally crisp and suspicious as he spoke.

"Are you saying that one of the heirs learned that Weldon was about to marry, thus depriving him of part of the estate? And learning that, poisoned him?"

Mercado spread his palms upward and achieved a graceful Latin gesture. "And what else?"

"Well," I said, "if one of the heirs killed Weldon, Palacios certainly didn't. I thought you implied there was some tie-up between the two murders."

"But, of course, there is. It is obvious. The person who poisoned Weldon hired Palacios to murder Colimo."

"But why? Why the devil should they want Colimo killed?"

"Because he would have conjured up Señor Weldon's spirit to talk to Mrs. Thackeray. The spirit would have told her how he was done to death."

"My God," said Washburn, "you don't believe all that mediumistic hooey, do you?"

"Does it matter what I believe?" asked Mercado. "The point is the killer believed it. Believed that Weldon's ghost would talk to Mrs. Thackeray."

It became clearer now. "So," I said, "you are arguing that either Weldon or Miss Hutton murdered Weldon, senior, then somehow found out that Mrs. Thackeray was going to consult Colimo. Believing in spirits, the killer was afraid Colimo would summon up old Weldon's shade and he'd make the accusation. So the murderer then hired Palacios to do the dirty work."

Mercado nodded. *El Coronel* looked slowly around the room. Palacios glared at him defiantly. The others seemed more amazed than guilty, with the possible exception of Ronald Weldon whose face was flushed, and in whose eyes there was anger.

"Are you saying," he demanded, "that I killed my father? Damn it, are you?"

"I am not," said Mercado flatly.

"Then who—" I began, and shut up as the full implication of Mercado's sentence came to me.

If one of Weldon's heirs had committed the murder, and if Mercado absolved Ronald, it left only the girl, Mary Hutton. This thought seemed to have hit everyone at the same time it had struck me. Now we all turned slowly and looked at the girl.

Her black eyes returned our gaze. "Have you any proof of this?" she asked Mercado.

"I shall have in a moment," he replied.

She smiled without mirth. "Have you any theory as to how I could force all those pills down my uncle's throat without his making an outcry?"

"You did not force them down his throat. I told you he took them voluntarily."

"Then," said *El Coronel*, "how the devil can you call it murder? If—"

Mercado sighed. "You are obtuse, *mi coronel*," he said, holding up the bottle again. "Look, I told you there was gum on the outside of the label. And the pills were in pink capsules instead of white."

"You've said that at least twice," said Washburn. "What the devil has that to do with it?"

"It is transparent," murmured Mercado. "You see, since the pills *looked* different it was a simple matter to convince Weldon that they *were* different. Miss Hutton told him that the doctor had prescribed different pills this time. She superimposed another label over the one the druggist had affixed—a label which called for four or five pills every half hour or so. So Weldon took the whole bottle in a few hours. He died."

I GAPED at him. It seemed simple enough A now. "And later," I said, "she merely washed off the phony label again."

Young Weldon looked at his cousin, said, "My God!" and shuddered. Washburn removed his glasses with trembling fingers.

I observed that the color had come back into the cheeks of Elsie Thackeray. She stared at the Hutton girl and there was bitter hatred in her gaze.

"I asked you once before," said Mary Hutton in a contained tone, "can you prove any of this, *señor?*"

"It is largely circumstantial," admitted Mercado. "But what does it matter whether I prove it or not?"

"A great deal," said *El Coronel*, looking worried again. "Against an American we must have a clear-cut case. If not, there will be an international, an international—er—"

"Stink?" said Mercado whose vocabulary ran the gamut from the gutter to the library.

"Stink," said *El Coronel* firmly. "You must prove she killed her uncle."

"Why is that necessary when we can prove she hired Palacios to murder Colimo?"

It is a difficult, even impossible, task to signal with only your eyes and facial muscles that you will give someone a vast sum of money to keep his mouth shut, yet that was the way I interpreted Mary Hutton's desperate glance at Palacios. However, he seemed to understand. He drew himself up.

"I shall say nothing," he said. "Save to issue denials. If I was seen at the scene of the Colimo killing, it is a matter of mistaken identification. Everyone is innocent."

El Coronel looked helplessly at Mercado, who remained blandly calm.

"I am sure he will talk," said Mercado. *"Amigo,* you forget *la ley del fugitivo."*

Palacios gulped. He had indeed forgotten the law of the fugitive and Mary Hutton had doubtless never heard of it. Recalling it, all the cash in Christendom was not going to keep Palacios' mouth shut.

In Mexico there is no capital punishment. And there are few killings committed for gain. Most of them are murders of passion, and purely personal. The average punishment for these crimes is something under eight years in prison. However, in blatant and brutal cases the police invoke *la ley del fugitivo.* It is effective, simple and not at all original.

It means simply that the criminal is shot dead on the steps of the police station while attempting to escape. Perhaps, he actually does attempt to escape sometimes, perhaps not. Anyway, it is a law from which there is absolutely no appeal. Mercado, in short, was threatening Palacios with nothing less than death if he did not implicate his accomplice.

REALIZING THAT we had him, Palacios turned with grave dignity to *El Coronel* and took the only course he could.

"I shall tell all, all," he said. "It is my duty as a citizen to aid the cause of justice. This woman hired me for fifty thousand pesos to kill Colimo. Though I do not know why."

Mary Hutton's pretty lips framed a dirty, ugly word. Then, as one of the coppers took her arm, she began weeping hysterically.

"The why was pretty obvious," said Mercado. "You'll recall that Miss Hutton predicted the end of the war. She said an Irishman named Doyle—A. Doyle told her. When I saw that Colimo ad, I realized she meant Arthur Conan Doyle, the great spiritualist who is now dead. She must have believed she had been in communication with his spirit. Naturally, I thought of Colimo. Half the American women in Mexico go to him."

"But how," I asked, "did Hutton know that Mrs. Thackeray was going to see Colimo?"

"That wasn't too hard. She either saw her name in the appointment book, as I did, or perhaps Colimo, unaware that they knew each other, mentioned it. Hutton did not dare let Colimo keep that appointment."

"But why," I asked again, "didn't she kill Thackeray instead of Colimo?"

"You ask me that?" said Mercado, a touch of bitterness in his voice. "It's a damned sight easier to get away with killing a Mexican in this country than an American. Dead Americans cause trouble."

At a sign from *El Coronel*, his two coppers escorted Mary Hutton and Palacios outside to the cars down the road. Mercado gazed reproachfully at *El Coronel*.

"I think," he said acidly, "I am entitled to the renewal of my pistol permit."

El Coronel nodded. "A thousand pardons," he said. "I shall issue the necessary orders when we return. Come, *amigo*."

We followed *El Coronel* down the road. Two questions still pounded in my brain. I gave voice to them.

"Look," I said, "I understand almost everything now. But why did that Thackeray dame pull that trunk business on me? Why did she hire a couple of muggs to swipe Weldon's body?"

"What else could she do? She had no status. She couldn't demand a post-mortem. She couldn't accuse anyone of murder. But she did want an investigation."

"But why did she play me for a sucker? Couldn't she have merely expressed the trunk to you?"

"It was easier her way. She was probably afraid of the Mexican Express Company. They have been known, quite often, to take weeks to deliver anything. By that time the corpse would be rather high. There would be an investigation. The body would be returned to Rayosso and sent home, still without any postmortem. No, she had heard of me, and wanted me to attend to the matter. She doubtless learned of your habit of breakfasting at Sanborn's and someone pointed you out to her. Moreover, she knew her melodramatic note attached to the corpse would interest me."

"All right," I said. "There's one more thing. What the devil were you doing in that cupboard in the kitchen?"

"Palacios got up to make his breakfast. There aren't many places to hide in that house."

"Suppose he had opened the cupboard door? He was armed. You weren't."

"I had to take that chance."

"But *why?* Why didn't you go over and wait in the hacienda as I suggested?"

"*Dios!*" he said. "It was raining. It rained ever since you left."

"So what?"

"Am I insane? I had no raincoat. To have ventured across the road in that downpour was to invite pneumonia. Do you think I am a fool?"

DEATH IN THE SUN

I HAD SEEN MARIANO MERCADO
FACE A THUG'S AUTOMATIC WITH
AN IMPASSIVE COUNTENANCE,
GRAPPLE WITH A MURDERER
THREE TIMES HIS WEIGHT,
BUT THE SIGHT OF AN
ENLARGED PHOTOGRAPH OF
THE MOST INNOCUOUS GERM IN
CHRISTENDOM, WOULD CAUSE HIM
TO TREMBLE IN ABJECT TERROR.
THUS MERCADO'S RELUCTANCE TO
THROW AN UNWELCOME GUEST
OUT OF HIS OFFICE—IT WOULD
HAVE NECESSITATED PHYSICAL
CONTACT WITH A HUMAN GERM
CARRIER. AND THE VISITOR
COULD NOT VERY WELL LEAVE
UNDER HIS OWN POWER WITH A
BULLET HOLE IN HIS BACK!

CHAPTER ONE
THE TATTOOED CORPSE

IT WAS winter but the birds sang songs of spring.
It was January but the sun shone brilliant and warm.
The palms in the *zócalo* were verdant and green. The air
was crisp and rare upon the mile-high plateau upon which
Mexico City is ideally situated.

We had just finished an unrationed lunch, Mariano
Mercado and I. I pushed away the remnant of Roquefort
left upon my plate; drained my cup of *café negro* and lighted
a cigar which would have cost three times as much back
home in the States.

I glanced across the table at Mercado. I was possessed
of such a sense of well being that for once his sartorial
splendor failed to outrage me.

Today, he was conservatively caparisoned—that is, for
Mariano Mercado.

His suit was a deep chocolate brown with lapels as broad
as a burlesque joke, as sweeping as a statement of Con-
gressman Rankin. His tie was a violent green and spotted
tastefully with saffron polka dots.

His vest was of merino wool but no sheep had ever been
born that color. It was of a yellow which would have caused
canaries to blink. His shoes were of the same hue, perhaps
a trifle darker. The topcoat which now reposed in the

An odd, gutteral sound
emanated from Dumbross'
throat. Then his knees buckled.
As he fell, I saw the spot
of blood at his temple.

checkroom was a delightful powder blue and his gloves a bright tan. His shirt, I forbear to mention.

The ensemble was, in a word, blinding. I take my oath that I have seen burros avert their heads when Mercado passed by.

The man who wore this regal raiment was a trifle under five feet tall. His skin was the color of old copper and his eyes were as shrewd and bright as those of a lynx. Now, he emptied his coffee cup, pushed back his chair and stood up.

"Well," I said, "what now?"

His gaze held mild disapproval.

"I am a professional man," he said. "These are business hours. I shall return to the office."

"For what? We have no clients at the moment. Nor any prospects. Why not spend this sunny afternoon sitting on the sidewalk in front of *La Cucaracha*, sipping *habanero* and watching the crowds go by?"

"You are a reckless man," he said.

"Why? *Habanero*, taken in limited quantities, won't hurt me."

"I do not speak of *habanero*," he said primly. "I speak of the people at the neighboring tables."

I knew what he was driving at. However, I pretended I didn't and lifted my eyebrows.

"What's wrong with them. Some of the best people in town—"

"I speak neither of their characters nor their social attributes." He bent over and brandished a brown forefinger under my nose. "What do you know of their diseases? What do you know of the bacteria they carry with them? How many of them are tubercular? How many afflicted with other ills? Heaven only knows what malady you may pick up mixing with crowds such as frequent *La Cucaracha*."

A fat individual seated behind him coughed loudly. Mercado jumped as if he had heard a machine gun. Hurriedly, he put his handkerchief over his nose and walked briskly into the street.

"Well," I said, leaving him on the corner, *"I'm* going over to *La Cucaracha."*

"I," he said over his shoulder, "am going for my atomizer."

He dashed off mumbling about the number of germs foisted upon him by the fat man who had coughed.

I sighed and went on my way. Mariano Mercado was, for the most part, a brave man. I had seen him face a thug's automatic with an impassive countenance. I had seen him grapple with a murderer three times his weight. But the sight of an enlarged photograph of the most innocuous germ in Christendom would send him cowering under his sanitary bed, trembling in abject terror.

Compared to him, the average hypochondriac was a reckless, addlepated fool.

I SAT down at a sidewalk table of the cafe and ordered my *habanero.* I sipped it slowly, letting the alcohol and sunshine permeate through my system. I ordered a second one. As I did so, something caught my eye. Something chaotic in color and shocking to the eye. It was Mercado and he had changed his shirt to a snappy pink number with little handworked scrolls on the collar.

"Sit down," I said. "I thought professional men remained in their offices during business hours."

"I need a drink," he said simply. He turned to the waiter and ordered one. He took a clean handkerchief from his pocket and a small vial containing a colorless liquid.

The waiter brought him a glass and a bottle. Mariano Mercado did not imbibe immediately. First he performed his rite of purification.

He uncorked the bottle and wiped its mouth carefully with the handkerchief. He then spilled three drops from the vial into the glass, and swabbed it with the handkerchief. Now that both bottle and glass were completely disinfected, he deigned to pour himself a drink.

He gulped down the *habanero,* set down the glass and looked around apprehensively as someone at the bar cleared his throat.

"What made you change your mind?" I asked. "Why did you suddenly decide you needed a drink?"

"I had a mild shock, *amigo.* And I need your help back at the office."

"My help?" Mariano Mercado didn't often need my help. "For what?"

"To get an unwelcome guest out of the office."

"Well," I said, "you're better at insult than I am, especially in Spanish. And if that didn't work you could have thrown him out, couldn't you?"

"You know how I dislike physical contact with strangers. Even a healthy man is a carrier of millions and millions—"

"I know," I said hastily, "and billions of bacteria. In a pinch you could have pulled a gun on the guy."

He smiled wryly. "I tried that. It didn't work."

I finished my drink. "You interest me," I told him. "Let's go over to the office."

We walked some five blocks to the building which held both Mariano Mercado's domicile and office. The flat, up a single flight of stairs was as bleak as it was sterile. Mercado permitted neither drapes nor upholstery. The furniture was of polished hard wood, constantly scrubbed in order that no germ could ever get comfortably settled.

The windows were screened and the floors were tiled and naked. No microbe-attracting rug had ever graced it.

Mercado led the way. He pushed the door open and with Latin courtesy propelled me in before him. I stood for a moment in the square room and saw, sitting on the far side of the desk, a man. He was a paunchy man whose features were of a definite Indian cast.

His hat was on the floor at the side of his chair. His head leaned against the back of the chair and he regarded me with glassy eyes.

"*Señor,*" I said politely, "this is the *casa* of the Señor Mercado. He does not wish you here."

The man continued to regard me. He did not speak. I turned to Mercado. "What's the matter with him? Is he deaf?"

Mercado flashed me a melancholy smile.

"You are wrong by only one consonant, *amigo.* He is dead."

"Dead? Of what?"

"Steel, *amigo.* There is a bullet in his back."

I gulped. I walked around to the rear of the pudgy man. Through the cane back of the chair I saw the crimson stain on his coat. I saw the blood on the floor behind his hat. I sat down and lit a cigarette.

"For God's sake!" I said. "Tell me about it."

Mercado's shrug was graceful and expressive. "*Pero,* there is nothing to tell. Save that we are private detectives. And we now have a mystery delivered right to us. Fitting, *no es verdad?*"

I laughed, not without bitterness. "Fitting? A corpse in your house? Your relations with the police department of this town are already strained. They're going to want something detailed in the way of an explanation."

"Lupa admitted him." Lupa was the cook. "He said he wished to see me. She permitted him to wait while she went to market. In the meantime, I returned. I found him."

"Like this?"

"*Sí*, like this."

"Who is he?"

Mercado shrugged again. "Would you mind searching him to find out? I prefer not to. Despite the fact that he is dead, the bacteria which doubtless infest him are not. Did you know that microbes can exist on a corpse for—"

"Well aware," I shut him off and approached the body with very little pleasure.

I went through him thoroughly, pocket by pocket. I found six paper pesos and seventy-five centavos in silver. I found a small dogeared prayer book with no inscription in it. I found nothing else.

I put the money and the book on Mercado's desk. He looked at them curiously but did not risk catching any dire disease by touching them.

"No identification," I announced.

Mariano Mercado was looking beyond me to the corpse. While reaching for his inside pocket I had disarranged his tie. One button of his shirt was open. Mercado's eyes focused on that point.

"Open his shirt. There's something blue on his chest. Looks like tattooing."

I loosened the dead man's tie and opened his shirt. In garish red and blue a tattooing needle had written over his heart: *Miguel ama Rosa.*

"Ah," said Mercado, "Miguel loves Rosa. This, then, is Miguel."

"Now," I said, "we know exactly as much as we did before. What do we do? Call the coppers?"

"We can't keep the body here. In this climate it would invite an epidemic."

"Not to mention an investigation. I'll put in the phone call. You invent the story that goes with the body."

I PUT the necessary call through to Colonel Gomez of the *policía*. Mariano Mercado continued to stare blandly at the body. He was a man given neither to heat nor hysteria save when he went forth to battle the bacterial hordes which he was thoroughly convinced would eventually destroy not only him but all the civilized world.

I had run into him accidentally in a cheap saloon and later had retained him at the behest of a friend of mine. The result was an offer of a job as his assistant—though heaven knows I didn't assist much in a practical sense. I was principally of use in securing American clients who, for provincial reasons, seemed to have more faith in a foreigner when he was aided by one of their own countrymen.

At the moment, Mariano Mercado was taking the presence of Miguel's corpse much more calmly than I. Colonel Gomez was no friend of ours. He resented Mercado because the little overdressed man was possessed of a keener mind than any in Gomez' department. Moreover, Mercado was not a man to be overawed by authority and Gomez was a man who used his authority to achieve just that.

The revocation and reissuance of Mercado's gun permit had reached the stage of high farce. When Gomez was annoyed at him he canceled it. When he was compelled to ask a favor he gave it back. The corpse of Miguel, I was sure, would result in another cancellation.

"Let us consider," said Mercado, "why a man should be murdered in my office. Obviously, he was sitting here alone awaiting my return."

"And," I said, "someone else came in and shot him in the back. It's at once as simple and difficult as that. So we can't get anywhere by sheer ratiocination."

A buzzer sounded from the hall. I went to the door reflecting that Colonel Gomez was moving faster than usual. I opened it and a man, obviously American, entered before I could stop him.

He nodded to me, then to Mercado. "I'm Charles Hendershot," he announced. "Perhaps, you've heard of me."

We had. Despite the fact that the city of Mexico possesses a population something in excess of a million souls, the permanent American colony is a tightly knit community. I had never met Hendershot but I knew who he was.

He had lived out near Chapultepec Park for about three years. He was a retired Wyoming rancher who had sold his vast holdings and come south to live in the sun. He had brought his family and some of his old hands and retainers with him. He dwelt in luxury on a huge estate and mixed very little with the night-club set which infests the metropolitan areas after dark.

He was a big man without being fat. His age I estimated at about fifty and his face was burned and darkened by the Wyoming wind. He bore himself with an aggressive air, tempered at the moment by a mild amazement as he stared at the figure of Miguel seated tranquilly in Mercado's antiseptic chair.

"Who's that?" he asked.

"Oh, that," said Mercado, as if deceased guests were a common occurrence in this household. "That is Miguel."

Hendershot glanced at him sharply. He seemed about to say something, then apparently changed his mind and asked instead: "What's the matter with him?"

"He's dead," said Mercado blandly.

"Good Lord!" said Hendershot. "And do you keep dead men in your office?"

"Only until the *policía* remove them," said Mercado apologetically. "And did you want to see me on a business matter, *señor?*"

But Hendershot was far more fascinated by Miguel than any business he may have had with Mercado.

"But how did he get here? Who is he?"

Mercado sighed. He patiently explained what he knew of the corpse. When he had finished, Hendershot eyed him oddly.

"But if this is true," he said, "how can you know his name? You never saw him before, did you?"

Mercado explained about the tattooing.

"Then," said Hendershot, "you have a problem. You can't really identify him. You don't know his last name, do you?"

Mercado conceded we didn't know Miguel's last name. For some peculiar reason, that seemed to appease Hendershot's curiosity. He sat down at the side of Mercado's desk and stated his mission.

"SEÑOR MERCADO, you have a reputation in this town as an honest and reliable man. For that reason I have come to offer you a commission."

Mercado nodded modestly. Hendershot continued.

"A friend of mine will arrive in Mexico City tomorrow. At *Buena Vista Estación*. After disembarking from the train, he will be driven to the airport. There he will take a chartered plane south. I want you to accompany him from the station to the airport."

"For what purpose?"

"My friend has a number of enemies. I want none of them to harm him as he passes through Mexico. You will simply meet the train and drive him to the airport. I shall supply the car. For this I am prepared to pay seven hundred and fifty pesos."

"I accept," said Mercado. "But is this all I am to know of your friend?"

"All save his name. That is Dumbross. Eric Dumbross."

"How will I know him?"

"He is a tall, gaunt man. He will disembark from the only Pullman car on the train. He will be carrying a bright yellow suitcase bearing his initials."

"And I am to protect him against what?"

Hendershot shrugged. "Against any harm. That's all I can tell you. But you must be alert and on guard during the entire journey."

Mercado nodded. Hendershot took out his wallet and began to count out several dirty notes. A Mexican dirty note, I may add parenthetically, is much dirtier than a dirty American dollar-bill. No notes are manufactured in Mexico itself. All are imported from the American Bank Note Company of the United States. Because of war time shortage, new Mexican money has not been printed in years.

Mercado watched the bills and shuddered. He said: "*Con permiso, señor,* I would prefer a check."

Hendershot seemed surprised. "I never heard anyone object to a cash transaction."

"There are less germs on a check," I explained.

Hendershot seemed even more surprised. However, he shrugged his shoulders, took a checkbook from his pocket and scribbled on it. He handed it to Mercado, shook hands with us both and took his leave.

Before Mercado could fold the check and stow it away in his wallet, the buzzer rang again. This time it was Gomez.

Gomez was a fat, indolent *hombre,* about one-third Indian. There was cigar ash on the lapel of his uniform and a spray of dandruff on his shoulders. He fixed a pair of black and suspicious eyes on Mercado. Mercado, doubtless thinking of his pistol permit, forced a smile and said affably: *"Qué tal, mi coronel?"*

Gomez grunted. He shifted his eyes to Miguel and said: "Is that the corpse?"

"Indeed, it is," said Mercado.

"How did it get here?"

Mariano Mercado sighed and once more told what he knew of the body. Gomez smiled without humor. He said: "And do you expect me, an official of the *policía,* to believe such a story?"

"No," said Mariano Mercado sadly. He opened his desk drawer and took out his automatic. "I suppose you will want this?"

Gomez nodded. He stretched out his hand and then withdrew it. "Perhaps not."

Now it was our turn to become suspicious. Gomez had never in all his checkered career done anything for nothing. The more pleasant moments of his life were spent in taking Mercado's gun away from him. Now he hesitated.

"Perhaps not," he said again. He paced up and down the room. He came to a military halt before Mercado. "A man just left here. It was Hendershot. A rich *Americano*. Perhaps he retained you?"

"Perhaps," said Mercado noncommittally.

"Perhaps, he gave you a big fee?"

"It may have happened that way."

"Perhaps it is worth two hundred pesos to you to keep your pistol permit? Since you have just collected a large fee you can certainly afford it, and maybe in discharging your obligation to your client you will need your gun, no?"

Mercado sighed. It was a neat holdup. Normally, he needed a gun as little as he needed all the atomizers and germ repellents which cluttered his desk. But now he had accepted a fee to protect Dumbross from whatever might threaten him. Though he knew little enough regarding the menace, his gun was certainly called for.

He nodded in my direction. "Give him two hundred pesos, Latham."

As I took the bills from my pocket, Mercado sighed. "Ah, the life of a *detective particular* is a hard one."

Gomez tucked the bills in his pocket and showed his teeth in a smile.

"This, of course," he announced, "is good for this time only. If you get mixed up with any more corpses it will be revoked—forever."

Mercado nodded. "In the meantime what about Miguel here?"

"I'll have it removed," said Gomez. The door closed behind him and I heard his heavy footfalls descend the stairs.

CHAPTER TWO
HENDERSHOT'S
DEAD INDIAN

THE MORNING came up like every other morning in Mexico City. The sun shone brightly on the snow-capped peak of Popo and the weather was of a type which the California Chamber of Commerce would have given its eyeteeth for.

I rose early, bathed, dressed and set out in a taxicab for the home of Charles Hendershot, where it had been arranged I was to pick up the car with which we were to meet Dumbross.

I tugged at the bell pull outside the huge wrought iron gates of the estate. I waited a considerable time for them to be opened. The man who admitted me was some fifty years old. His cheeks were the color of red copper. His eyes were black and penetrating. I knew he was an Indian, but there was nothing either Aztec or Mayan about him.

I said to him in Spanish: "You're an American Indian, aren't you?"

He grinned at me revealing perfect teeth. He answered in English as good as my own. "Sure. From Wyoming. I used to work on the Hendershot ranch. The chief brought me along with him when he retired. Are you the guy from the detective agency?"

"I'm the guy."

"Come along with me to the garage. I've been told to give you the sedan."

We walked along a tree-lined gravel path to the enormous garage at the rear of the house. I noted there were four cars in it as we entered.

"You've got a lot of cars," I said. "And a lot of room in that house, too."

The Indian nodded. "We need them. Mr. Hendershot brought me, his old foreman and all his family down with him.... Take that car there. The Buick sedan."

I climbed in and stepped on the starter. The Indian rode down to the gates with me, let me out and relocked them. I drove the car back to Mercado's office and picked him up there.

He wiped the upholstery carefully before he climbed in. Then, despite the spring temperature, he closed all the windows as a precaution against drafts and any loose germs which might be riding on the sunbeams.

We parked outside the station and went in to wait for the train. We waited. The National Railways of Mexico are not celebrated for promptness. We waited for ninety minutes, dropping into the bar from time to time to wet our throats with tequila. Mercado, of course, went through his bacteria-killing ritual before each drink.

The station was filled suddenly with steam and pandemonium as the train from the north steamed in. Mercado and I dashed through the gates and stood waiting outside the door of the rear car which was the only Pullman.

The fourth passenger to get off was a tall, gaunt man. His cheeks were sunken and dark rings encircled his eyes. He was clad in a black cape and a black fedora hat. In his thin, white hand he carried a pigskin bag initialed *E.D.*

I stepped forward. "Mr. Dumbross?"

Dumbross conceded his identity in a deep, melancholic voice. I introduced Mariano Mercado. Dumbross apparently knew all about the arrangements. He accepted my explanation without comment and accompanied us out to the sedan.

On the way, I reached out my hand to take his valise. He shook his head and, it seemed to me, gripped the bag more tightly with his emaciated fingers. He got into the rear seat of the sedan. I took my place behind the wheel. Mercado, I observed, loosened his coat in order to be able to reach his shoulder holster easily if necessary.

From *Buena Vista Estación* to the airport is about a thirty-five-minute ride if the traffic isn't too bad. Usually in Mexico, it's too bad. However, we got through the town itself with no difficulty and hit the road to the airport.

I drove a little beyond the main entrance to the field, as several other cars were parked there. Mercado got out on the right-hand side of the car, the side away from the field. I got out on the left side. Mercado held the door open for Dumbross who stepped onto the running board on the same side as Mercado.

As I rounded the rear end of the car, Mercado's head was less than six inches from the gaunt face of Dumbross. Still gripping his bag tightly, Dumbross put one foot on the ground, then seemed to hesitate. His head jerked back. An odd, guttural sound emanated from his throat. He remained absolutely immobile for a split second.

Then his knees buckled. As he fell, I saw the spot of blood at his temple.

"Dios!" said Mariano Mercado as he dropped to his knees and lifted Dumbross' head. He closed his eyes and cursed quietly. Then he stood up. I stared at him in bewildered inquiry.

"Dead," he said. "A bullet through the brain."

My mind refused to accept it. I stared off to my right. There was nothing there save a fence which encircled a field. There was nothing in sight. Some seven hundred yards away a lazily revolving windmill was the only object that broke the flatness of the view.

"It's impossible," I said. "There wasn't anyone about to shoot him. Moreover, I didn't hear any shot."

Mercado nodded. "A high-powered rifle. Perhaps with telescopic sights. It could have been fired from the top of that windmill. That's why you didn't hear the shot. That's why you didn't see anyone."

"Well," I said, "let's get out there. Maybe we can catch up with the *hombre*."

He shook his head sadly. "He's out of the windmill and off through that tall grass. We'll never catch up with him."

Mercado paused for a long moment and sighed heavily. "I have bungled an assignment," he said sadly. "And I am out two hundred pesos."

That was true enough. Gomez was going to come very close to apoplexy when he discovered us with another inexplicable corpse. Mercado was most certainly going to lose his pistol permit again.

"Go ahead," he said resignedly. "Call Gomez. I'll watch the body."

I WENT into the airport and made the call. Less than half an hour later, a huge limousine pulled up alongside our sedan. Gomez disembarked with three of his aides.

Mariano Mercado was waiting with his gun in his hand. Holding it by the barrel, he tendered it to Gomez.

"I have another corpse," he said sadly, "and this time I don't have two hundred pesos to spare. I suppose you will want this."

Gomez snatched the weapon. He stared down at the dead body of Dumbross, then lifted a pair of angry eyes to Mercado.

"And this?" he demanded. "How do you explain this?"

"He was shot," said Mercado. "In the brain."

"And I suppose you have no idea who shot him?"

Mercado shrugged. "None."

I interposed hastily and explained what little we knew of the killing. When I had finished, Gomez shook his head sadly.

"Very well," he said. "Go away. Both of you. Wherever Mercado is, there is also trouble."

I climbed in behind the wheel of Hendershot's car and drove back to Mercado's office. I followed his dejected figure up the stairs into the room where he sank, sighing, into the chair behind his desk.

"It is a most interesting case," he said. "I wonder if Hendershot will pay us to solve it?"

"That I don't know," I told him. "However, you'd better cook up some bright tale to tell him. When I return the car I'll have to let him know what happened. He will not be pleased."

"The difficulty is," said Mercado, "that Hendershot, in all probability, knows something which would aid us. I do not think he will talk. He didn't when he engaged us. He undoubtedly knows what was in the bag."

"What bag?"

"Why, the bag Dumbross carried."

I puzzled over that one for a while, then thought I understood.

"So, you opened his bag while you were waiting in the car for the police to arrive?"

Mariano Mercado shook his head. "No," he said. "I tried and could not do so. That is why I know he carried something important. Probably he carried the thing for which he was killed."

"You're a little enigmatic," I said. "However, at least the killer didn't get the bag."

"I'm very much afraid he did."

"But it was right there in the car when Gomez arrived."

Mariano Mercado brought a sigh up from the very soles of his tiny feet. "Was it?" he said and lapsed into a brooding silence.

This nettled me. "Will you kindly tell me what you're talking about? I'm referring to the bag again."

"Oh, the bag. Well, when I was sitting in the car, I thought I should open the bag. Perhaps it would contain some clue to the killing. So I took a bunch of keys from the corpse. None of the keys would fit."

"So?"

"It is as obvious as pneumonia. The bag must have been switched. Certainly Dumbross would have carried the key to his own bag."

"But how? Why?"

"That I do not know. You will return the car to Hendershot and ask him if he cares to pay us to find out."

"Do you think he'll care to engage our services again after we fumbled the first assignment?"

Mercado nodded. "I think perhaps he might. Since he is an American, he will have a very low opinion of the Mexican Police Department. Moreover, there are not many private operatives in town. None who speak English grammatically. And I rather think Mr. Hendershot will be most interested in finding out who has Dumbross' bag—even more interested than in having someone indicted for murder."

I got up and sighed. "All right," I said. "But frankly, I don't think much of the assignment."

His dark eyes narrowed. "Wait a minute," he said.

I waited, while he stared at the bare and antiseptic wall.

"Look," he said at last, "you know that lottery store across the street?"

"I should. I keep them in business."

"You know Pancho?"

"Sure."

"Well, he's there all day leaning over that counter and thrusting his busy nose into whatever happens. Ask him if a truck or some sort of wagon pulled up in front of here yesterday. Just after we got back from lunch."

I blinked. "Why?"

"Just ask him."

It was my turn to shrug. I turned on my heel and left the room.

I went across the street, bought a lottery ticket and asked Pancho Mercado's question.

"*Ayer?*" he said. "Yesterday. *Á las tres horas?* There was no truck. No cart. *Pero,* there was a station wagon. It went away after a little while. Why?"

Since I didn't know the answer to that myself, I said nothing, recrossed the street and climbed once more into the Hendershot car. I drove off slowly. I was in no great rush to face Charlie Hendershot. I was sure he wasn't going to like the news I had for him.

I BRAKED the car at the iron gates which led to the Hendershot estate, climbed out and tugged at the bell.

After a short wait my old pal, Indian Joe, arrived, grinned at me and opened the portals. He climbed into the front seat beside me as I drove around the house to the garage at the rear.

As I came out of the garage I said: "Is Mr. Hendershot in? I want to see him."

The Indian looked at me oddly, I thought. Then he shook his head. "He's downtown. But he should be back soon. Do you want to wait? I'll introduce you to his nephew. Come on."

We walked toward the house. The Indian stopped suddenly and stared into the sky. Curiously, my eyes followed his gaze. I peered into blue sky, nothing more.

"What is it?" I asked.

"Buzzards. Way the hell up."

I stared again. I still saw nothing but sky.

"I can't see any buzzards."

The Indian chuckled. "You will in a minute."

I kept on staring. A few second later I saw two black pinpoints in the heavens.

"I see them now," I said. Then added: "You have damned good eyes."

He nodded proudly. "The best in Wyoming. I can see anything that—"

A querulous voice interrupted us. "Bill, you talk too damned much. Who is this gentleman?"

I turned around. Standing some few yards from us, beneath a huge bougainvillaea, was a thin pale-faced individual of about thirty. He was well-dressed, and smiled mirthlessly at me in greeting.

Bill explained my identity and my mission. Then he announced to me that this was Walgreen Phillips, Hendershot's nephew.

"Come on up to the house," he said. "My uncle should return soon. In the meantime you can have a drink. You, Bill, get back to the caretaker's lodge."

I watched the glance the two exchanged and came to the conclusion that there was no great friendship between the Indian and Hendershot's nephew.

Phillips led me into the house. A few moments later, I was seated in a cushioned chair of which Mariano Mercado would have vehemently disapproved. Doubtless, a trillion germs had taken up their abode in the luxurious upholstery. However, it was comfortable.

Phillips brought me a Scotch and soda and chatted amiably. As we talked, a square-shouldered man with gray hair and a weathered face came into the room.

He said: "Where's the boss? Did Dumbross get through all right?"

I squirmed uneasily in my chair. Although the Indian had told Phillips who I was, I had not yet mentioned Dumbross. I only wanted to make that speech once and I was saving it for Hendershot.

Phillips shrugged. He said to me: "This is Hamilton. Used to be my uncle's foreman in Wyoming. He's still his right hand." Then he looked back at Hamilton and said: "Latham here can tell you about Dumbross. He's just returned the car in which he drove Dumbross to the airport."

Hamilton looked at me inquiringly. There was nothing I could do except tell the truth.

"Dumbross," I said, "is dead. He was shot through the head as he got out of the car at the airport."

HAMILTON INHALED swiftly. He stared at me as if he were holding me personally responsible for the murder.

"Shot?" he yelled. "I told Hendershot not to engage any damned fool local shamus. My God, where is he now?"

"You mean Mercado?"

"I mean Dumbross."

"The *policía* have taken over."

"And have they got—" He broke off. "Where have they taken him? Whom should I see?"

"Colonel Gomez. He seems to be in charge."

Hamilton cursed again and ran from the room. I gathered he was dashing to the garage for a car. Phillips seemed to have taken the news more or less quietly.

"Did they get the guy who shot Dumbross?" he asked.

I shook my head. I emptied my glass and began to wish that Mercado had handled this deal himself. A few moments later, Phillips got up. He said: "There's my uncle now."

I heard a door slam and a moment later, Hendershot entered the room. Phillips greeted him, waved a farewell to me and left us alone. Hendershot said: "Well?"

I stood up, took a deep breath and went into it. As I was finishing my story, Hendershot's face became an angry red. Before he could speak, I said hastily: "Mr. Hamilton has already gone down to the police who have the body and effects. And Señor Mercado wants to know if you would be interested in retaining him to help find the killer."

"Mercado!" he cried and it sounded very much like a dirty word.

He stared at me. He opened his mouth as if to ask a question then appeared to think better of it. As we stood there in silent and unpleasant tableau, Phillips raced into the room.

"Come with me!" he yelled. "They've got Bill. He's out in the back there, by the new chicken run. He's dead."

Hendershot blinked. Then, without a word, he ran after Phillips who raced out of the house, across the back lawn. I took a deep breath and dashed along after them. At least, I reflected, here was one corpse which Mercado wouldn't have to explain.

We ran over mowed grass, through a thicket of palm trees into a barren area where some concrete had been laid. We were forced to climb over a barrier of carpenter's horses and various tools in order to reach the space where the Indian lay.

He was on his back staring into the clear blue Mexican sky. As we came up to him I saw that there was a crimson stain over his heart. Hendershot looked down at him. He clapped a hand to his brow distractedly.

"For the love of heaven!" he cried. "Why, Bill? What on earth did Bill have to do with it?"

He knelt down at the Indian's side and touched his pulse. The Indian opened his eyes which surprised me. He certainly should have been dead by now. He apparently was a tough Indian who died very slowly.

He looked at Hendershot, then at me. Finally, his gaze traveled to Phillips. He shook his head slowly, then spoke in such a low tone I could scarcely hear him. He said, as closely as I could make out: *"Yo semiti."*

Then he closed his eyes. Hendershot shook his head. "My God! Why would they do this? Why—"

He caught my eye. "All right," he said. "Get Mercado. I need all the help I can get. I've heard he's a bright boy, though the Lord knows he certainly didn't demonstrate that fact today. Tell him to work on the case. I'll pay him a fat fee. But it's contingent. If he doesn't deliver he doesn't get paid. And there's one other thing."

"Yes?"

"When and if he finds this killer I want him delivered to me personally. Not to the coppers. I want him handed over to me. Do you get that?"

I nodded.

"All right. Go get him. There isn't any time to lose. The trail's getting colder every minute."

CHAPTER THREE

MESSAGE FROM GARCIA

I **TURNED** on my heel and left the estate. I found a taxi out in the street and after the usual spirited haggle, engaged it to take me back to Mercado's office.

I found him poring over a statistical pamphlet issued by an insurance company. He looked up as I came in. There was a worried expression on his face.

"Do you know," he asked, "how many Indians die from *pinta* each year in Patagonia?"

"No," I said. "However, three men have died from bullets within the past twenty-four hours. One right here in this room, one whom you were supposed to be guarding at the airport, and now Hendershot's Indian."

He blinked his black eyes mildly, said: "Hendershot's Indian?"

"Yes. I told you about him. Well, he just got a bullet in his heart out at Hendershot's place."

He sighed, ran his slim fingers through his raven hair and looked contemplative.

"Moreover, Hendershot's decided to retain you, on the condition that you hand the killer, if and when found, over to him—not to Gomez."

Mercado nodded slowly. "That checks with what I've been thinking. He really doesn't want the killer at all."

"Then why is he offering you dough to find him?"

Mariano Mercado glanced at his wrist-watch. He seized a blue bottle from the array on his desk, tipped a pill into his palm, placed it on his tongue and washed it down with a sterilized glass of triple-distilled water.

"All right," he said, "tell me about it. Tell me all that you know. And in English. You think better in your own language."

I lit a cigarette and went into it. I related every pertinent item which had occurred during my visit to the Hendershot establishment. I finished with the story of the dying Indian's last words.

"He looked at me, then at Hendershot, then at Phillips. Then he said, '*Yo semiti.*' Of course *yo* is Spanish for *I*. But I'm damned if I can figure the verb. What does it mean?"

He stared at me for a long, silent moment, then said: "What does it mean in Spanish?"

"Naturally."

He sighed. "Nothing."

"But it must mean something. A dying man doesn't talk jargon."

"It does mean something. But not in Spanish. The man was an American Indian, you know, not a Mexican Indian."

"Well, it certainly doesn't mean anything in English," I said testily.

He smiled faintly. "You have been wrong before, *amigo.*"

For the time being, he let it go at that. A few minutes later, we went out for our leisurely lunch. We had returned to the office for the siesta period, but before I could divest myself of my coat there were racing steps on the stairs and a sharp knocking at the door. I opened it to admit Hendershot.

His eyes blazed with fury and his cheeks flushed. He brushed past me into the presence of Mariano Mercado.

"That Colonel Gomez," he exploded. "He's a crook. A thief. A swindler."

Mercado bowed gravely and in wholehearted accord. "*Es verdad,*" he said. "He is all of those things. And more."

"You've got to do something about it," roared Hendershot. "I'll pay you any reasonable price. But you've got to help me."

"What did *el coronel* do?" asked Mercado.

"Swindled me. I went to see him. I wanted to get Dumbross' effects, to send them to his relatives back in the States. Well, in order to cut red tape I offered Gomez a thousand pesos if he'd give me Dumbross' baggage."

"And he failed to do so?"

"He gave me the baggage all right. But he'd been through the valise first."

"You mean he'd stolen something from the bag?"

"He certainly had!"

"What was it that he stole?"

Hendershot opened his mouth and closed it again. "I happen to know," he said quietly, "that Dumbross carried something of great value in his bag. It isn't there now. Gomez has stolen it."

Mercado shook his head slowly. "I have a low opinion of Colonel Gomez. It is difficult for me to defend him.

Nevertheless, *señor*, he did not steal anything from the Dumbross' bag."

"But it's not in the bag now," said Hendershot. "And I know he was carrying it when he arrived in Mexico."

"True," said Mercado. "But whatever it was, it was taken from him on the train. I think that someone switched bags on him."

Hendershot stared at him incredulously.

"You see," Mercado explained patiently, "while I was waiting for the police to come for the body, I began to wonder. I felt rather responsible for the killing. I thought perhaps I might find some clue to the murder in his bag. So I took the keys from the corpse and tried to open it. None of the keys fitted."

Hendershot frowned. "But that's impossible. Dumbross certainly had a key for the valise."

Mercado nodded. "That's what I thought. It seemed strange that he should travel with the locked bag and no key. So I reached the conclusion that his bag had been switched for another which, externally, looked about the same."

HENDERSHOT LOOKED at him keenly. "Go on," he said, "keep talking. I'd heard that you were a bright boy."

"It came to me," went on Mercado, "that perhaps whoever switched bags on him wanted Dumbross dead before he discovered what had happened. Why? Because when Dumbross opened the bag, he would know at once who had made the switch. So he was killed at the airport."

"Anything else?" said Hendershot. "It sounds all right so far."

"Possibly there is some more," said Mercado. "But, as yet, it's all conjecture. I couldn't prove any of it."

"Can you find the murderer?"

"I think I can find him. But whether I can produce enough evidence for a conviction is something else again."

"I don't want evidence. I want him."

"You are going to punish him yourself, *señor?*"

"No. The police may have him when I'm done with him. I want him first. And I won't need the kind of evidence that a court will need."

Mercado smiled blandly. "Naturally. As a matter of fact you don't want the killer at all. You merely want to get your hands on the valise."

There was a long silence. Hendershot stared thoughtfully at Mercado. "You are a bright boy after all, aren't you?"

Mariano Mercado nodded a reluctant assent.

"*Con permiso,* I shall come out to your house this evening. There are some things I want to look into. There are some questions I desire to ask."

"All right," said Hendershot. "But let's not waste any more time. The killer could be in Siam by now."

"I think he will remain in Mexico City," said Mercado. "Until tonight, then."

Hendershot stalked out of the office. I looked at Mercado in complete bewilderment.

"What's it all about?" I asked. "Have you really any idea?"

He spread his palms. "I have several ideas. I can almost explain precisely what happened. But I lack one fact. I do not know the exact motive. And I know nothing of Dumbross. Now, let us have a half hour's silence. I must think."

I picked up a magazine and immersed myself in it as Mariano Mercado gave himself over to thought. About twenty minutes later, footfalls sounded on the stairs. I answered the knock at the door to admit Gomez and a slim, mustachioed man of about thirty.

They followed me into Mercado's presence. "This," announced Gomez pompously, "is Señor Garcia. He is a confidential agent of the Federal Government."

Mercado bowed. Gomez sat down heavily. He looked around the room expansively, made a gesture in Garcia's direction.

"Ask him, *señor*. Ask him what we want to know."

Garcia regarded Gomez coldly. "You will leave us, *coronel*. I wish to speak to this *hombre* privately."

Gomez blinked. "But I am of the *policía*."

"Privately," said Garcia adamantly.

Gomez got up. Disgruntled, he left the room. As the door closed, Garcia said: "That one, I do not trust."

"Nor I," said Mercado. "Your business, *señor?*"

"You were with this Dumbross today when he was murdered?"

"I regret to admit that I was."

"And it was the *Americano* Hendershot who engaged you to travel to the airport with Dumbross?"

Mercado didn't answer right away. He stared at Garcia and his bright little eyes became brighter. "Wait a minute," he said. "Maybe this is it. Perhaps, it has fallen right into my lap. You are Garcia, a confidential agent of the Federal Government. Interested in political matters, maybe?"

Garcia nodded. "That's right. So I've come here to find out what you know about Dumbross."

"Perhaps," said Mercado, "it will be mutually advantageous if you tell me what you know instead."

Garcia shrugged. "Not much. His name was not Dumbross and he was an agent of the Falangist Party of Spain. That much I know. I suspect that he was traveling through Mexico to another country to foment a Fascist revolution."

Mariano Mercado smiled beatifically. "I love you," he said simply.

Garcia started. I hastened to explain that this was merely Mercado's method of signifying whole-hearted approval, nothing more.

"I love you," he explained, "because you have provided me with the missing piece of my puzzle. If what you say is true, could it be possible that Dumbross was carrying a large sum of money in his bag to be used in furthering his political plans?"

"It would be quite likely. Save that Gomez assures me he wasn't carrying any luggage at all."

"Gomez lies. He sold his bag to Senior Hendershot."

Garcia stood up. "Then let's get the bag," he said excitedly. "Perhaps there's something in it. Perhaps—"

"There isn't," said Mercado wearily. He went into an elaborate explanation of his switched valise theory.

Garcia nodded as he finished. "I am not particularly interested in what money he may have had in his bag, or the fact that it was stolen from him. Dumbross has been stopped. But I want his accomplices."

"If you will come to Señor Hendershot's home with us tonight," said Mercado, "I can deliver them to you. You may have to dig up your own evidence. I also think I can have a killer or two for Gomez. I need my gun back."

"Your gun back?"

Mercado sighed and explained his difficulties with Gomez.

"Don't worry," said Garcia. "I'll get you back your gun. Tell them at the house I'm a helper of yours. It won't be necessary to tell them my official position."

"I don't get it," I said. "Do you expect to find Dumbross' friends and his killer all at Hendershot's place?"

"I do," said Mariano Mercado.

"Then I still don't get it."

MERCADO DIDN'T answer me. He looked over the array of bottles on his desk and selected those pills, antiseptics and various other nostrums which he thought he might need before the night's work was done.

He stuffed them in his topcoat pocket and then, despite the mildness of the night, carefully donned it, wrapped a white silk scarf about his thin neck, pulled on a pair of woolen gloves and announced he was ready to foray forth.

We were ushered into the Hendershot living room by a white-coated Indian. A fire burned brightly in the vast grate. Seated before it were Phillips and Hamilton. Hendershot rose from a desk as we entered.

Mariano Mercado introduced Garcia as his second assistant. I gathered that the implication was that I was his first. Then we all sat down while the servant mixed us a drink. Mercado rose once and closed a window some four yards away from which there was no draft whatever. Then he sighed and said: "This is a bad business."

All of us watched anticipatorily. I knew him well enough to know that he really had something. There was a suppressed excitement about him. For the moment I doubted if he was even aware of the bacteriological peril which constantly threatened all mankind.

"Well," said Hendershot, "go ahead with your questions. When will you be able to turn the killer over to me?"

"Before the evening is over," said Mercado, He bowed in Garcia's direction as if tacitly making the promise to him at the same time, "First," he went on to Hendershot, "you will forgive me if I clear up the matter which most concerns me. For that I would like you to call in the servants."

"The servants? What on earth can they have to do with it? They're all ignorant peons who couldn't possibly understand what is involved here."

"Nevertheless, will you call them, *por favor?*"

Hendershot shrugged and spoke to the butler. He disappeared and came back a few minutes later followed by an awed group of six people, three of them women.

Hendershot said: "I'll give you their names and positions."

Mercado shook his head. "That is not necessary."

He stood up and approached the huddled group. He smiled at them, said: *"Qué tal, amigos?"*

They bowed and smiled back at him uncertainly.

"I am your friend," he said. "I am your good friend. I come to bring you news of Miguel."

The response to that crack was amazing. Six voices rose in concert and cried: "Miguel?"

"Indeed," said Mercado. "You were his friends?"

They nodded in unison. A woman of about forty detached herself from the group. "I was to marry him, *señor,*" she said. "I am the cook, Ulalia. I have been *triste* since he disappeared, *muy triste.*"

"Of course," said Mercado, "Miguel was interested in politics? Interested in his country's welfare?"

"*Sí, señor.* I have told him politics was not for an ignorant peon such as he, but he would not listen. But tell me, señor, where is he? What has happened to him?"

Hendershot said: "What nonsense is this, Mercado? What has this to do with what I am paying you for? This is idiotic. Back to the kitchen, all of you."

"*Espere!*" snapped Mercado and his voice cracked like a whip, The servants halted.

Mercado crossed the room. He put a consoling hand on the cook's shoulder. "I regret, *señorita,* that your lover is dead."

The woman burst into tears. At a signal from the butler, the other servants led her from the room. Mercado sighed and resumed his chair. He sat still and silent, gazing thoughtfully into the fire.

Phillips, Hamilton and Garcia were staring at him.

Hendershot glowered, and said: "What the devil are you up to?"

"The matter in which I was most interested," said Mercado, "was naturally the murder committed in my office. That was what I wanted to check first."

Hendershot grunted. "And now have you checked it?"

"Indeed."

"And what have you learned?"

"I have learned nothing. I have merely corroborated what I knew from the beginning."

"And that is?"

"That you killed Miguel."

CHAPTER FOUR
IT'S IN THE BAG

THERE WAS a long silence. Phillips and Hamilton looked somewhat incredulously at Hendershot.

Hendershot said: "Are you *loco?* Why the devil should I kill an eighty-peso-a-month gardener?"

"First, let me tell *how* you did it. You came to my office and found Miguel there waiting for me. He had come to tell me of Dumbross—who the man was, and what he was about to do. Miguel was a democrat and a patriot. He does not approve of the Falangists. So you killed him in my office.

"You left immediately to get a conveyance in order to remove the body before discovery. When you came back with the station wagon, I had already returned. So you pretended you didn't know Miguel. It was safe enough. You'd taken all identification from his pockets. And who cares about a dead peon? The newspapers don't even mention such killings. It was a hundred-to-one that no one at this house would ever hear of the killing even if they read the papers, which they don't."

Hendershot licked his lips. "And how did you know that I knew Miguel?"

"Because you were so concerned when you learned that we knew his first name. You were terrified that you had overlooked some identification which would have established his last name as well as his first. Then he could have been traced to this house."

"And," said Hendershot, "to establish a case you must also supply a motive for my killing him, you know."

"That is not too hard, even if it is only conjecture. You, *señor*, are a Falangist. It was your task to see that Dumbross was protected while going through this city. To that end, you planned to engage me. Miguel must have overheard you talking of it to Hamilton or your nephew. Miguel did not approve. He decided to call on me first to tell me what was afoot."

"You can prove this in a courtroom?" said Hendershot.

Mercado shook his head. "I am only trying to convince my friend, Señor Garcia here."

"I am convinced," said Garcia grimly.

"Then let us move on to other matters," said Mercado. "Now let us get to the murder in which you are interested— that of Dumbross."

"Of course," said Hendershot, not too convincingly, "this talk about my killing Miguel is absurd. I am glad you concede that you can't prove it, Mercado. But get to Dumbross."

"Dumbross," said Mercado, "was killed by a man about whom I can furnish no proof, either. However, in this case it doesn't matter."

"What the devil do you mean by that?" said Hendershot. "It certainly matters whether or not you can produce proof in the Miguel affair."

Mercado shook his head dreamily. "Oh, no, it doesn't," he said.

"Proof or no proof," said Hamilton moving uneasily in his chair, "we want the man who killed Dumbross."

"You'll have to dig him up," said Mercado. "By the way, where is he buried?"

"Who?" snapped Hamilton.

"Your Indian. Your American Indian. Bill, I think he was called."

Hendershot and Hamilton gaped at him. They said, almost in unison: "You mean that Bill killed Dumbross?"

Mercado nodded. Phillips blinked at him and, for that matter, so did I. How he had masterminded this was, at the moment, utterly beyond me.

"I have ceased to think you a bright boy," said Hendershot. "Bill didn't know what it was all about. He could have had no possible motive for killing Dumbross. He didn't even know who Dumbross was."

"He killed him for what was in that bag," said Mercado.

Hendershot took a deep breath. "You mean Bill switched those bags? He couldn't have. He was here on the estate almost all morning."

"Look," said Mercado mildly, "perhaps, it will be easier if I first tell you who killed Bill. Then we can work backwards."

"Very well," said Hamilton, "who killed Bill?"

Mercado looked around the room and at last his black eyes lighted on Phillips. "He did," he said.

PHILLIPS RETURNED his gaze steadily for a moment, then he threw back his head and roared with laughter.

"This is good," he said. "The entire household is a nest of killers. First, Uncle Charlie killed Miguel. Next, Bill killed Dumbross. Then I killed Bill. Who has Hamilton murdered?"

Mercado spread his palms. "I have no idea," he said. "But that doesn't concern us."

Garcia turned to him anxiously. "You're sure of all this?"

Mercado nodded. "Surest of all that the men you want are Hendershot and Hamilton. Gomez will want Señor Phillips."

Hendershot said: "This is becoming a farce. Either you have cards, Mercado, or you haven't. If so, play them. Whom are you accusing and what is your evidence?"

"Bill is dead," said Mercado. "Hence I am accusing you of killing Miguel and your nephew of killing Bill."

"You've already given us the Miguel theory. What is this about my nephew killing the Indian?"

"It is simple and obvious. Your nephew was one of the people who knew of Dumbross' arrival?"

Hendershot nodded.

"And he also knew what was in that valise?"

"Yes, he knew."

"So what is simpler? He takes a taxi or perhaps one of your excellent cars and drives north to Barrientos or Lecheria or some other nearby town. There he boards the train. He doubtless knew from you what Dumbross would look like and what sort of bag he would be carrying. Your original information must have contained those items so that Dumbross could be identified when you sent me to guard him.

"So, Phillips had a substitute yellow bag made. It wouldn't have to be too exact a facsimile. The chances are Dumbross would not notice as long as the bag had the general characteristics of the original."

I glanced at Phillips. It was apparent that he possessed neither the stoicism nor the guts of his uncle. His face was pale and there was frank terror in his eyes.

Mercado continued: "It was simple enough for Phillips to inform Dumbross that discretion prevented you, Hendershot, from meeting him. Your nephew conveyed your greetings and then slipped off the train alone as soon as it arrived at *Buena Vista Estación*. Now Phillips had the bag. But sooner or later Dumbross would know that they had been switched. Moreover, it wouldn't be too difficult to figure out who had done it. So it was necessary to murder Dumbross."

There was blazing fury on Hendershot's face as he turned to his nephew. Phillips stammered: "He can't prove it. He's making it up just as he made up that yarn about your killing Miguel."

"Of course," said Mercado, "I knew this was what had happened but I did not know who had switched the bags until this morning—that is, until after your Indian, Bill, had died."

Hendershot looked back at Mariano Mercado. "What has that to do with it?"

"The man who killed Dumbross fired the shot from a windmill a thousand kilometers away. Either he used a telescopic sight or he was possessed of uniquely splendid vision. Now, since the war such sights have been absolutely unobtainable in Mexico. The American Indian is reputed to have the eyes of an eagle. He—"

I thought of something. "He had!" I explained. I told of Bill's sighting the buzzards in the sky before I could even see them in pinpoint size.

"Naturally," said Mercado. "He was Phillips' accomplice. Phillips stole the bag. The Indian killed Dumbross. Apparently they were to split the swag."

There was a moment's silence in the room. Never in all my life had I seen such an expression of flaming rage as was on Hendershot's face at that moment.

"But," said Hamilton dubiously, "how can you know Phillips killed the Indian? You weren't even near here at the time."

"Why," said Mercado blandly, "the Indian himself accused Phillips. Before witnesses—Hendershot and Latham, here."

"That," said Hendershot, "is a lie."

Mercado shook his head. "What did Bill say when he died?"

"*Yo* something," said Hendershot. "Evidently he spoke in Spanish. I caught the word *yo*. I missed the verb."

"There was no verb. And there were not two words. There was only one. The word he spoke as he stared at Phillips was *yosemite*."

"Yosemite?" I said, "that's a national park in the States."

"Sure," said Mercado. "Remember Bill was an American Indian. In death he reverted to his natural language. Yosemite is an Indian word. It has two meanings. The first is grizzly bear."

"And the second?" asked Hamilton.

"Killer," said Mariano Mercado.

I watched Hendershot. It seemed to me that some of his wrath was abating, that there was a thoughtful, crafty expression in his eyes.

"It's all conjecture, said Phillips anxiously. "Don't believe him, Uncle Charles."

"It will cease to be conjecture," said Mercado, "when your fingerprints are found on the bag."

HENDERSHOT TRANSFERRED his attention from his nephew and gaped at Mercado.

"You mean you know where the bag is?"

Mariano Mercado nodded. He lit a brown cigarette. "Look," said Hendershot, "tell me where the bag is and name your own price."

Garcia said: "You really can locate the bag?"

Again Mercado nodded. "I shall deliver it to you, *señor*. It would do you no good, Hendershot. Remember, you must be punished for the murder of Miguel."

"Rot," snapped Hendershot. "You have no evidence there at all."

Mercado smiled faintly. "We don't need any. The men of Colonel Gomez have a most simple system. Since we have no capital punishment in Mexico, since a man's life is never taken by the law, it is amazing how many of them try to escape. No, Garcia?"

Garcia smiled without mirth. I knew what he was talking about. True, there is no capital punishment in Mexico. An ordinary murder of passion will get you something from two years to ten. However, a killing of which the police disapprove for reasons of politics or morality will get you a bullet in the back. The official announcement will state that you tried to escape.

I looked up at Hendershot. From the pallor on his face I realized he was aware of all this.

"First, and most important," said Garcia. "Where is the bag? The Government will want it."

"Well," said Mercado, "Latham here tells me that the Indian was killed out at the edge of the estate where some construction is going on, a place quite inaccessible and a little difficult to reach. One must, I am told, climb over carpenter's horses to get there. So—"

He broke off as Hamilton got to his feet and pulled a .38 from his hip pocket. Hamilton backed to the fire-place and covered us all with the gun.

"O.K.," he said. "I get it."

Mariano Mercado smiled and waved a palm. "You see," he said to Hendershot, "you had a bright boy in your employ all the time."

Hendershot said to Hamilton: "What the devil are you talking about?"

"It's easy to figure what he's going to say next. Bill was killed out in an inaccessible spot. What was he doing there?"

"He was hiding the bag," said Hendershot.

"Close," said Mercado. "He was digging it up."

"Of course," said Hamilton. "He and Phillips had hidden it out there. Bill decided on a doublecross. He went out to get the bag. Phillips caught him at it and killed him. Then Phillips dashed in here and said he'd found Bill shot."

Hendershot drew a deep breath. "We haven't lost yet, then. Hold them here. Keep that gun on them. I'll get some of the servants and a couple of shovels and find that bag if we have to dig all night. It must be somewhere near the spot we found the body."

Hamilton nodded. "After that we can lock 'em up and take the bag out of the country ourselves."

"Sure," said Hendershot from the doorway. He glared at Phillips. "Except for him."

I thought for a moment Phillips was going to faint. He was quite aware that a tacit death sentence had been passed upon him.

HENDERSHOT LEFT the room. We heard his footsteps fade away down the long corridor. Phillips buried his head in his hands. Garcia looked at Mercado. Mercado heaved a heavy sigh, glanced over at me and raised his eyebrows.

I knew what he meant and I didn't like it. Some time ago we had agreed that when a situation similar to this occurred we should simply advance on the man with the gun from two directions simultaneously. It meant that one of us, quite likely, would get shot. But the man with the gun would lose it.

Mercado leaned forward in his chair. He was still smiling blandly. I braced myself and was aware of a strange emptiness at the pit of my stomach. I made no bones about the fact that I was as afraid of bullets as Mariano Mercado was of germs.

Mercado's voice cracked out. *"Adelante!"*

I sprang from the right and he hurtled through the air from the left. Rattled, Hamilton swung his gun's muzzle to Mercado, then hesitated and swung it around to me. I closed my eyes but kept going.

I opened them as I heard the sound of shot. I saw the gun shoot a hole in the ceiling as Hamilton went over backwards. Garcia had attacked from center and reached his objective with his head in the middle of Hamilton's stomach.

Hamilton fell screaming into the fireplace. Mercado seized his fallen gun.

Mercado said: "Garcia, have you a gun?"

"Naturally."

"Take these men in. Latham and I will get the bag."

Garcia prodded Phillips to his feet. I followed Mercado into the garden.

A lantern bobbing ahead of us in the darkness guided us. We approached silently, Mercado in the lead like a stalking cat. We came upon them as Hendershot, far too engrossed to hear, was staring down into an excavation in the earth just beyond the line of newly-laid concrete.

Two of the manservants were digging. Just as we came up, one of them lifted a dirt-stained pigskin bag.

"*Es este, señor?*"

Hendershot grabbed the bag as Mercado poked the gun in his ribs and said: "*Con permiso.*"

He snatched the bag with his left hand. Hendershot turned around and wilted. The taller of the two servants leaped from the hole and put a hand on Mercado's throat. I slugged him and he fell.

Mercado handed me the bag. "Tell the peons to go to bed. We don't need them. We have the bag and Hendershot."

I spoke to the servants in Spanish. The man I had hit got up slowly and crossed himself. As he did so the yellow gleam of the lantern shone on his hand. Mercado stared at it and his face turned from coppery brown to tattle-tale gray.

"*Dios!*" he exclaimed. "*Mire!*"

I looked. There was something of a blemish on the man's right hand.

Mercado howled, "Ringworm! I am dead."

He dropped the gun. Hendershot and I grabbed for it. I won by a millimeter and thrust its muzzle into his ribs. Mercado was thrusting trembling hands into his pockets. One of them emerged a moment later with a tiny bottle of iodine. The bottle slipped in his hands and dropped on the concrete.

"*Dios!*" he shrieked. "And where will I find a *farmacia* open in this neighborhood? *Dios!*"

He had completely forgotten the matter in hand. He turned and fled into the night, racing down toward the main gate in search of a drugstore. I cursed him, sighed and took Hendershot back to the house.

I arrived at the Mercado domicile some two hours later. Mercado sat at his desk. Although his hand was red with iodine he was soaking it in a colorless solution.

"Listen," I said, annoyed, "when you dropped that gun, Hendershot could have snatched it and killed us both."

"Does it matter whether I die from a bullet or a disease? I *had* to get a disinfectant."

"So I noticed. We opened the bag."

He evinced a little interest. "What was in it?"

"Dough. Two hundred grand in American notes. He must have smuggled it across the border. Plus several political documents mentioning names which will not only interest the Mexican Government but also the American State Department."

Mercado sighed. "I should be given a pension," he said. "I have risked my life for my country."

"So did Garcia and I," I said. "We tackled Hamilton while he held that gun, too."

"Gun," he said contemptuously. "Who cares for a gun? But were you touched by a peon with ringworm? Was Garcia? Do you know what I have risked? Here, let me give you the statistics."

I sighed. I settled back and lit a cigarette. I got the statistics. In Spanish, in English and in detail.

A TOAST TO THE KILLER

"IT IS MOST URGENT, *SEÑOR*," SANCHEZ TOLD MARIANO MERCADO. "MY COUSIN IS WOUNDED. HE IS NOW IN THE HOSPITAL AND I WANT YOU TO STAND GUARD OVER HIM." MIGHT AS WELL ASK A MAN TO JUMP OFF A ROOFTOP AS TO SUGGEST THAT MERCADO EXPOSE HIMSELF TO SUCH DANGERS OF DISEASE AND INFECTION. HOWEVER, THERE WAS A FAT FEE INVOLVED—WITH WHICH THE LITTLE LATIN SHAMUS COULD BUY MORE ANTISEPTICS AND PANACEAS—AND THE CASF PIQUED HIS CURIOSITY. THE PATIENT WASN'T BADLY WOUNDED, YET HE SHOWED NO SIGNS OF GETTING WELL. WHO COULD—WITH A SCALPEL PIERCING HIS HEART?

CHAPTER ONE
ASSAULT AND FLATTERY

AS A man who has dwelt in both countries, I am quite willing to concede that the citizens of the United States are more able in several respects than their Mexican brothers. They are, like Mussolini, capable of keeping the trains running on schedule. They possess an incredible mechanical ingenuity. In the matter of sanitation they are superb.

However, I state categorically, they have no idea of how to eat their lunch. When the hour of noon strikes in New York, Chicago or Los Angeles, the huge granite buildings vomit forth the hordes of workers who dash frantically to a drugstore counter and hastily shovel an unappetizing tuna fish sandwich down their dull and undiscriminating palates.

This tasteless treat is topped off by a slab of apple pie, created on the assembly line of a huge bakery, and a cup of coffee as spiritless as a slave and weaker than the mind of a retarded bobby-socker.

Now say what you will about the Mexican, but, *por Dios*, he certainly knows how to partake of his *comidas*.

First, he waits until half past one to make absolutely sure that he is really hungry. Then he deliberately locks his office or shutters his shop and ambles to his favorite restaurant. There he partakes of two or eight *habaneros,* the number depending on his desire and his capacity.

Following that he sits at a table surrounded by his male cronies and proceeds to knock the living hell out of nine full courses, washing them down with liberal drafts of tequila, *vino tinto* and whatever other refreshment is at hand.

Following this he emphatically does *not* go galloping back to his place of labor and proceed to waste his life in toil. He goes home, repairs to his bedroom and spends the next two hours in good solid sleep. And if that isn't civilized, brother, I will eat Mr. Buckle's book on the subject.

The man's pajama coat had been pulled back and there was a neat incision directly over his heart. Blood stained the sheet and the man's chest.

On this particular September day, the brilliant sun shone down upon the plateau where Mexico City is situated. The sky was clear and the air was crisp. In the distance the twin peaks of Popocatepetl and Ixtaccihuatl reared their snowcapped heads to the heavens. And the faintest breeze slid gently over the highlands from Acapulco.

I was lunching at Minuit with Mariano Mercado. Despite the fact that it is one of the best restaurants in North America, Mercado outraged the waiter by taking a large silk handkerchief from his pocket and wiping each piece of silver individually. He then applied the same procedure to every piece of china. Completing this ritual he deigned to glance at the menu.

He ordered a lengthy and elaborate lunch and since I was his guest and had no worries about the check I did

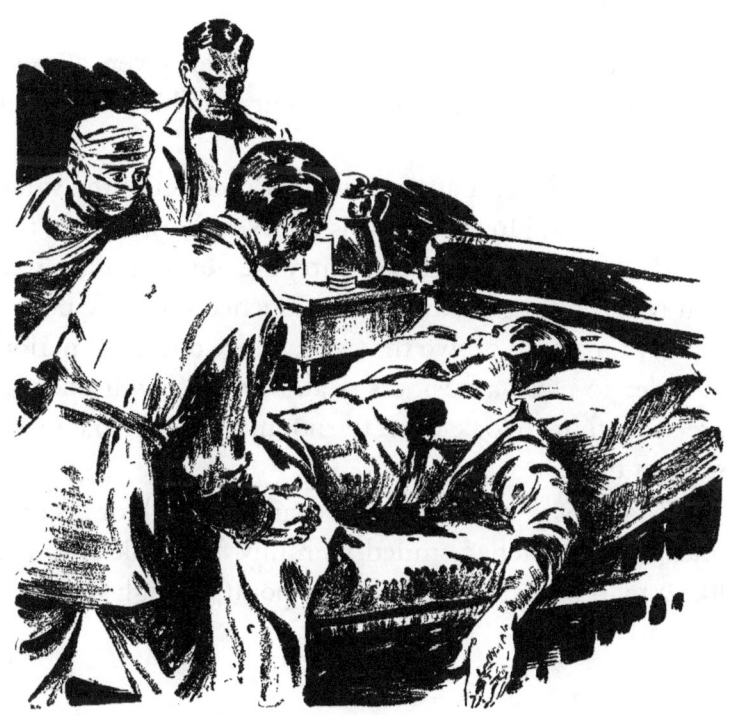

the same thing. We were halfway through a thick steak when a little dumpy man wearing a pair of black-rimmed glasses approached diffidently and stood at Mercado's elbow.

Mercado halted his fork in midair and turned his dark, liquid eyes on the stranger. Among the several million things which irritated him, being interrupted as he ate was one of the major items. He lowered his fork slightly and said: *"Qué pasa?"*

The stranger said, with a nice touch of awe in his tone: "You are Mariano Mercado?"

Mercado's stern face relaxed somewhat under this subtle flattery. He nodded his head admitting his identity.

"My name," said the stranger, "is Pedro Sanchez. I would like very much to retain you. I am in need of your valuable services, *señor.*"

MERCADO PUT down his fork. Clients were all very well in their place which was, of course, in his office after the siesta hour.

"Señor," he said, "I appreciate your opinion of the value of my services. However, this is not New York City of the *Estados Unidos.* We of this country are not so money mad that we grub for gold during our luncheon. We are not so hungry for a peso or two that we sacrifice our siesta period in order to close a business deal. My office will open at precisely four o'clock this afternoon. I shall be happy to see you then."

He made a gesture of dismissal and reached for his fork once more. Sanchez smiled painfully. He looked to me like a man prepared to argue the point, though most reluctantly.

"Don Mariano," he said, laying it on with a trowel—it was as if he had called him "revered sir" in English—"time is of the essence. I will pay you for your time, two thousand pesos, *señor.*"

Mercado looked at him sternly. "And will money repay me for a ruined digestion? For an illness brought about by my failure to rest after my meal? Remember, señor, Mariano Mercado is not a gringo businessman."

Sanchez shuffled his feet uneasily. *"Pero, señor,"* he said, "you may save a life if you come with me after lunch. I want you to meet a friend of mine. He is wounded. He is in the hospital. I want you to stand guard over him."

"In a hospital?" Mercado shuddered. "Heaven only knows what germs dwell in a hospital. Think of the poor creatures suffering from heaven knows what diseases who are lying there. There are not enough pesos in all Mexico, *señor,* to impel me to guard a man in a hospital. *Dios,* and who would guard Mercado?"

Sanchez look bewildered. "Guard you from what, *señor?*"

"From the host of bacteria in your hospital. From the frightful carriers of disease dwelling there." Here he put down his fork. "Let me give you some statistics, *señor.*"

At this point I rushed into the conversation, I knew by heart all the vital statistics Mercado was about to cite. I was in no mood to hear these depressing tables again, especially while I was eating.

"Señor Sanchez," I said, "if you will return to your table I shall do my best to interest Señor Mercado in your proposition before he concludes his meal. I shall communicate with you before we leave the restaurant."

Sanchez nodded. Then he said something which proved that either he was a far shrewder operator than I had suspected or else was possessed of execrable taste.

"*Gracias,*" he said to me. He turned to leave, swung his head around again and spoke to Mariano Mercado. "If you will forgive me, *señor,* I must ask you a personal favor before I leave. Could you give me the address of your tailor?"

Mercado beamed. He fancied himself as a combination of Beau Brummel, Adolph Menjou and Lucius Beebe. Actually his taste in raiment was that of a colorblind Hottentot.

"Certainly, *señor.*" He took a card from his pocket and handed it over. He added: "I shall stop by your table on the way out and listen to the details of what you have to tell me."

Sanchez beamed back at him and left us. Mercado thrust a huge chunk of meat into his maw and cocked a triumphant eye in my direction.

"You heard that?" he said. "You heard him ask for the name of my tailor. Have I not told you that my clothes appeal to the eye of the man of fashion. You North Americans have no feelings at all for color."

If I had any feeling at all for the color of the outfit Mercado was wearing at the moment, it was a feeling of nausea.

His suit was cut sharply, with lapels that almost reached down to his hips. Its hue was something between saffron and mustard. His shirt was greener than the Amazonian jungle and his socks held more motley shades than the prism is aware of.

His shoes had buttons instead of laces and were of two tones either one of which is better left unmentioned. But the item on which he had completely run riot was his tie. No poet dosed with hasheesh could have done justice to the Mercado cravat. The background was a delicate puce and superimposed on that was every color, every hue, every pastel and tint of which the human mind could conceive. A bird of paradise would have taken one single look at that tie and killed itself.

This sartorial degeneration was, however, his minor vice. His major difficulty was his utter and complete hypochondria. I had seen him face a thug's gun as gallantly as an infantryman at Okinawa. I had seen him fling himself at a weaving hand wielding a knife and wrench it from the killer's grasp.

But I had also seen him run howling from a room when someone coughed. I had seen him cower in a corner when approached by a peon with ringworm on his wrist. For Mariano Mercado feared a germ like a felon fears the gallows.

His pockets, his bureau, and his desk drawers were filled with lotions, antiseptics, pills and various other armament with which to combat the bacterial hosts against whom he was constantly waging war. He knew the names of more diseases than a medical dictionary and was armed with more statistics than the Johns Hopkins library.

Nevertheless, he had a keen mind and save for these two obsessions, was the sanest man I had ever met. Our original meeting had been completely fortuitous. Later, I had thrown a case in his lap, at the successful conclusion of which I had been retained as his assistant.

There wasn't a great deal of money in it. But then one doesn't need a great deal of money to live comfortably in Mexico City.

I DID some thinking over the dessert and by the time we had reached our liqueur and cigars I had come to the conclusion that two thousand pesos was a reasonable offer for the giving up of a siesta.

"Look," I said, "why don't you snap up Sanchez' proposition?"

"I shall. If he calls on me at my office in the proper manner and at the proper time."

"But he says it's urgent. He apparently wants us to go out to this hospital immediately. That's why he's offering such a fancy fee."

"It's not fancy enough to compensate me for the lost of my post-prandial rest."

I sighed. I knew this was going to be hard. But I didn't completely share Mariano Mercado's complete disregard of money. It was several weeks since we had had a client and I was not as glib in Spanish as he was when it came to appeasing landlords and divers other creditors.

A happy thought came to me.

"Look," I said, "with your cut of that fee do you know what you could do?"

"What?"

"You could buy a new suit, a half dozen ties and several bottles of vitamin pills or iodine or whatever you think you need most for you health."

He frowned thoughtfully. I knew he was weighing the loss of the siesta against the ghastly colored fabrics available only at his tailor's, against the surging war he could conduct against bacteria with fresh drugstore ordnance.

At last he sighed. "I shall doubtless regret this," he said. "However let us look into the Señor Sanchez' proposition."

I stood up and led the way to the table where Sanchez was dining in solitude.

He sprang to his feet as we approached. He pulled out Mercado's chair and, beckoning the waiter, ordered three of the most expensive cordials in the house.

He said eagerly: "Have you decided to accept my fee?"

"There is such a possibility," said Mercado. "If you will be kind enough to acquaint us with the details."

Sanchez blinked owlishly behind his glasses. "There isn't much to tell you save that my cousin, Juan Sanchez, was attacked last night as he was returning to the house where we live together. He was shot in the shoulder and left lying in the gutter for dead.

"He was taken to the hospital where he is now. I am afraid for his life. He may be attacked again in the hospital. The assassin may return to finish what he started."

Mercado frowned skeptically, said: "Do you know of any reason why someone should shoot at your cousin?"

Sanchez shook his head. "None at all. He is a simple man. A pharmacist. He has no enemies that either he or I know of."

"Then why," asked Mercado, "should you fear that someone would climb through the hospital window and shoot him again?"

Sanchez shrugged. "I have a premonition," he said blandly.

Mercado lighted a cigarette. Incredulity still glittered in his dark eyes. "I understand you want us to watch over your cousin while he is in the hospital. And after that? When he returns to his home?"

"I still want him guarded."

Mercado grunted. "And for two thousand pesos we must watch over your cousin for the rest of his life?"

"Oh, no, *señor.* After he leaves the hospital I will pay you one thousand pesos a week as long as you watch him. It will be for not longer than two weeks."

Mercado clapped a hand to his head. He started to say something, then closed his mouth. I squirmed uneasily on my seat. Experience had taught me that he was a most temperamental *hombre.* I was terrified he was going to turn down a thousand pesos a week.

Rather to my surprise he said: "The matter begins to interest me. Mr. Latham, my assistant, will go with you to the hospital. He will guard your cousin until such time as he goes home. Then I shall help him."

"Good God, Mercado," I said, "I don't mind working, but that guy may be in the hospital for a month or more. Am I supposed to stand a continuous shift?"

Mercado shrugged his little shoulders. "A clean bullet wound in the shoulder shouldn't keep him there long. He will be able to leave in a few days, I am sure."

"But I can't stand a single shift for two or three days. I've got to get some sleep."

"I have observed," said Mercado acidly, "that you manage to stand two-day shifts in certain unsavory *cantinas.*"

"Look," said Sanchez, "come and see my cousin, *señor.* Come now. I believe he is able to leave the hospital this very day. But he is afraid. He thinks he is safer there so he desires to stay. But once he sees the elegant, the brave Mariano Mercado, once he knows that Mercado will guard him at his own home he will no longer be reluctant. But come and see him. Reassure him."

Mercado expanded under the flattery. For a moment he looked as if he were going to accede without further argument. Then he frowned suddenly.

"*Pero,* a hospital! I can't venture into a hospital!"

"Don't be an idiot," I told him. "What is more sanitary than a hospital? No one is more hygienic than a doctor and hospitals are full of them."

"Certainly," said Mercado. "But they wear gauze masks, rubber gloves and sprinkle themselves with disinfectants."

"Only when they operate," I said. "Come along."

He wrinkled his brow again and appeared to be doing some heavy-duty thinking.

"What hospital?" he demanded.

"Santa Cruz."

"*Bueno!*" said Mercado with satisfaction. "I know a surgeon there. I must see him first."

To this minor concession both Sanchez and I eagerly agreed.

CHAPTER TWO

CURE SUCCESSFUL— PATIENT DEAD

W E WENT out of the restaurant into the bright sunshine of the *Paseo de Reforma.* We stood for a moment at the edge of the wide tree-lined boulevard in the shadow of the immense statue of *El Caballo Bronce,* waiting for a taxi.

I hailed one at last and Mercado engaged in the customary spirited haggle with the driver, who eventually deigned to drive us to the hospital for two pesos.

Once there, Mercado insisted that we go ahead into the ward where Sanchez' cousin was bedded while he called upon his friend the surgeon. At the entrance to the ward we met a dark and diminutive nurse.

"*El Señor* Sanchez sleeps," she informed us. "Shall I awaken him?"

"Not yet," I said. "Since we have to wait for Mercado, we may as well let him sleep until he gets here."

Sanchez nodded assent. We sat down in a pair of reed chairs and waited for Mercado. We waited a full fifteen minutes.

At the end of that time a figure, which I took to be that of a doctor on his way to the operating room, approached. His head was completely covered by a gauze cap. A mask of the same material swathed his face. The rest of his body was covered by a long white robe and his hands were encased in a tight-fitting pair of rubber gloves.

He swept through the corridor like an apparition and halted before the chairs where Sanchez and I were seated. A muffled voice sounded behind the mask.

"Well, where's his cousin?"

I blinked and stared for a moment at the familiar pair of black eyes visible above the

"My God!" I said. "Mercado! What in heaven's name are you doing in that get-up?"

"Am I to risk my life for two thousand pesos? Would a diver descend into the ocean without his protective helmet? Would a soldier go into battle without his tin hat? Should I enter this germ-infested hive without adequate protection? Now where in Satan's name is his cousin?"

Sanchez and I stood up. "He's asleep," I told him. "However, we'll get the nurse to awaken him."

I beckoned the nurse who, firmly believing that Mercado was a senior surgeon, bowed politely and led us through the ward. She stopped at a bed almost in the center of the room, with, perhaps, five other beds on either side of it.

There a man lay on his back, his head twisted on the pillow. He bore a marked resemblance to Pedro Sanchez, though his coffee complexion seemed to be more diluted. His cheeks were as pale as a dark skin can possibly get.

The nurse touched his shoulder. *"Señor,"* she said in a hissing whisper, *"Señor, aquí están su amigos."*

Juan Sanchez did not move. She shook him this time with no result. *"Señor,"* she said loudly. *"Señor!"*

I leaned forward and looked more closely at the man. I observed that his eyes were open, staring blankly at the ceiling. I felt my pulse pick up a beat.

"Mercado," I said, "look at—"

But he had already seen it. He pushed the nurse aside, reached for the man's pulse, then remembered he was wearing gloves. He hesitated for a moment, then began to remove the rubber covering from his right hand. He thought better of it. If a life was to be risked it might as well be mine.

"Latham," he said, "feel the man's pulse."

I put my finger on the wrist which lay outside the bedspread. There was no pulsating reply. I caught Mercado's eye and shook my head. At my side Pedro Sanchez was staring at his cousin and there was something strongly resembling fear in his gaze.

Mercado spoke to the nurse. "Summon the doctor in charge. This man is dead."

She spread her palms. "But how can it be? He only had a bullet wound in his shoulder. There was no fever. How could he die?"

"We shall see," Mercado mumbled behind the gauze.

He bent over and pulled back the covers. The man's pajama coat had been pulled back and there was a neat incision directly over his heart. Blood stained the sheet and the dead man's chest.

There was a tight silence for less than three seconds. Then the nurse's ear-splitting scream shrilled into my ears.

"He's dead," she cried. "Murder! And in my ward. Dios, what horror!"

"*Vàyase,*" snapped Mercado. "Get Doctor Meana. *Apúrese!*"

Shaken, the nurse ran from the ward. Sanchez put his hands on the window sill to steady himself. Mercado, muffled up like a mummy, had a thoughtful expression in his eyes.

A few moments later, the little nurse returned with Dr. Meana, Mercado's friend, in tow.

He bent over the bed, examined the body.

He straightened up and shook his head. The little nurse made a vehement Latin gesture of despair. She pounded a fist against her breast and said: "*Dios!* Murder! What a horrible thing!"

She buried her face in her hands and began to weep.

"*Sí,*" said the doctor to Mercado. "It is murder, indeed. He has been stabbed through the heart with an exceedingly sharp knife or perhaps a scalpel."

I glanced over at the living Sanchez. There was an odd expression on his face. It seemed to me that he was registering half shock and half relief.

Mariano Mercado's keen black eyes looked around the ward. He walked over to the window behind the bed and peered through it.

He said to the nurse: "I suppose any ambulatory case in this ward could have killed him? Also, anyone could have leaned over the window sill."

She lifted a tear-stained face. *"Sí,"* she said. "I myself saw half a dozen of the ambulatory cases talking to him during the exercise period."

Mercado sighed and nodded. To the doctor he said: "Let us go to your office where I shall divest myself of my protecting garment."

We left the sobbing nurse and the ward behind us and adjourned to Meana's office which was off the main lobby near the hospital entrance.

AFTER CAREFULLY closing the door against any angry germ which may have followed him, Mercado removed his mask. He peeled off his rubber gloves and struggled out of his white robe which, I may add parenthetically, was the most conservative piece of apparel ever to drape his torso.

"Well, Latham," he said to me, "your avarice, your quest for gold has brought me to this. I have given up my siesta, I have risked my digestive system. And for what? To gain two thousand pesos for guarding a man. The man, it appears, is dead. So I cannot guard him. So I do not collect two thousand pesos."

"But," I said, glancing at Sanchez, who was standing by the window lighting a cigarette, "if the señor was willing to pay you two thousand pesos to watch over his cousin, he certainly would be willing to pay you more than that to apprehend his murderer."

"Quizá," said Mercado. We both cast a look of inquiry at Sanchez.

He turned from the window, met our gaze and spread his palms in a tolerant gesture.

"I am not a vengeful man," he said. "As long as I may protect the living I shall do so. But a dead man cannot be restored to life. If his killer is found he will be punished. But that will not return my cousin to me. No, it is God's will. I shall do no more in the matter."

Mercado looked at him reproachfully. I knew quite well that I would not hear the end of this. My gringo greed was going to be loudly blamed for depriving Mercado of a health-giving siesta.

"*Señor,*" I said "surely you have more family feeling. The incompetent police will never find the killer of your cousin. But the Señor Mercado, here, is a bloodhound when he takes the trail."

I laid it on, heavy and thick, for a good five minutes. But the Señor Sanchez wasn't having any.

"No, *señor,*" he said. "If a man is ill, is hungry or is in trouble I shall help him. If he is dead he is beyond my help. I am not interested in the killer of my cousin."

Behind us, Dr. Meana hung up the telephone after concluding the call he had just put in to the police department. At that moment there was a knock upon the door.

The doctor said: "Come in."

The door opened and Juan Ibanez entered. Juan Ibanez was Mexico City's Walter Winchell. He was a tall man and the exceeding darkness of his complexion made it clear that his blood was almost pure Indian. He was dressed in a conservative gray suit which brought a sartorial sneer to the face of that distinguished man of fashion, Mariano Mercado. His face was thin and intelligent, his eyes alert. And his ears, in a figurative sense, stretched out over the entire capital. If Juan Ibanez hadn't heard of an event, in all probability it hadn't happened.

He nodded to us and bowed deeply to the doctor. "Ah, Meana," he said, "now what is this about a killing in one of the wards in your hospital."

A frown creased Sanchez' brow. He whispered to me. *"Quién es este hombre?"*

I told him, sotto voce, who Ibanez was.

Meana said, in annoyed surprise: "How can you have known about it so quickly?"

Ibanez showed his white teeth. "I have my agents everywhere. I pay them for tips. I have someone, who must remain anonymous, right here in your hospital, Doctor. He phoned me a few minutes ago."

Meana shrugged. "Well, since the police have been called, I suppose all the papers will have it anyway."

"Es verdad," said Ibanez. "But my paper will have it first. Now exactly what happened?"

"Let us get out of here," said Mercado. "My bed is lonely."

He moved toward the door but before he could open it, Sanchez spoke, urgency in his tone.

"Is this story to be in the newspapers?" he asked. "Why? My cousin was no celebrity. He was a simple man. He had neither money nor position. There are a hundred unmentioned killings per month in Mexico. Why should my cousin's receive publicity?"

Ibanez beamed at him. "Because of the circumstances, *señor.* A hospital is a place for repairing injuries, not aggravating them. If a man is murdered in a hospital, where he came to get well, that is news. Is it not? I shall plaster this upon the front page. Now, Doctor, what are the details, *por favor?"*

Meana sat down at his desk and proceeded to give the newspaperman what little details he possessed. Sanchez, who suddenly appeared greatly concerned, drew Mercado over to the window.

"Look," he muttered, "I have changed my mind. I shall retain you. I shall offer you more than two thousand pesos. I shall—"

"Good," I interrupted. "This is a sensible thing. You want the Señor Mercado to run down your cousin's murderer?"

"Partly that and partly something else. Listen, I shall tell you—"

Mercado held up his hand and shook his head decisively.

"You will tell me nothing," he said. "Not now. You will call on me at my office in two hours as is fitting and proper. I have delayed my siesta. I do not intend to lose it altogether."

"No," cried Sanchez, "I tell you—" He broke off as a thought seemed to occur to him. To Ibanez, he said: "When will your story be printed, *señor?*"

"It will be on the newsstands about eight o'clock tonight."

"*Está bueno,*" said Sanchez. He turned to Mercado. "I shall call at your office in two hours, *señor.*"

He walked out of the office. A moment later, Mercado and I followed suit. I dropped off at my hotel while Mercado went on to his combination office and apartment to rest himself before continuing his incessant onslaught against his bacteria foes.

I, too, lay down for about an hour. Then I rose, shaved, bathed, and dressed myself. After that I set out for Mercado's place on the *Calle de Maddelin.*

I felt quite pleased with myself. I didn't pretend to understand Sanchez' about-face but he had promised us more than the original two thousand pesos and I, at least, was certainly in a position to appreciate my cut of the money.

I CLIMBED the stairs to Mercado's apartment and let myself in with my own key. Apparently, he had just dressed himself. He was seated at his desk staring moodily at the phalanx of bottles on the blotter. After some cogitation he selected one, dumped two pills in his hand and washed them down his throat with a glass of triple-distilled water.

Then he reached for an atomizer and sprayed his larynx with care and thoroughness.

He put down the atomizer and said: "There is one thing I'll hand to you gringos. You are sanitary. Almost every American family takes vitamins, buys hundreds of bottles of disinfectants a year. Ah, if only Mexico spent as much money in their drugstores."

I said: "There's some excuse for my countrymen. They are constantly bombarded by advertising copy which implies that their children will die of a horrible disease if they don't use a certain brand of toilet paper. Their doctors tell them that if they eat normally vitamins are not necessary but the doctor's sane voice is unheard in the thunder of the advertising agencies. More American intestines are ruined by laxatives than Mexican intestines are wrecked by amoebic dysentery. Yes, there is an excuse for my countrymen being a nation of hypochondriacs, but what possible reason have you?"

He looked at me reproachfully and shook his head sadly. This subject was a constant bone of contention between us. He leaned backwards and took an awesome volume from the bookshelf. He said: "Let me give you some statistics."

I shuddered, said: "No. Let's discuss our client and our case and how we shall spend the fee. But, *por favor,* no statistics."

He sighed and replaced the book. "In your grave you will regret not having listened to me, *amigo.*"

"On that I'll gamble. Now, have you any idea who killed Sanchez' cousin."

He lifted his eyebrows and narrowed his pupils. "A vague idea but only a vague one. There were two rather peculiar things I observed in the hospital."

"Namely?"

"Sanchez' attitude struck me as extremely odd. I mean, of course, the living Sanchez."

"You mean when he changed his mind about retaining us? Hell, that was my eloquence!"

"Amigo," he said gravely, "you are never eloquent in Spanish. Your accent has heavy Brooklyn overtones. No, Sanchez' change of mind had something very definitely to do with Ibanez and the fact that the story of his cousin's death was to receive some publicity."

"That's reasonable. What else did you notice?"

"That I had better not mention yet. It is so vague it is ephemeral. On such a slight point I can make no accusation until I am absolutely certain."

I knew better than to press him. When he didn't want to talk he would remain stubbornly silent. He remained uncommunicative until there was a knock at the door. I opened it and admitted Pedro Sanchez. He looked far more worried than he had when standing over his cousin's corpse.

He said: "I am offering you more money now, *señor.*"

Mercado lifted his eyebrows. "Payable whether I find your cousin's killer or not?"

Sanchez nodded.

"*Sí,* provided you carry out the other part of the assignment."

"Which is?"

Sanchez drew a deep breath. A frown wrinkled his brow. He seemed most undecided. At last he sighed heavily and said: "Well, I suppose I must tell you."

"That seems an intelligent idea," said Mercado dryly.

Sanchez ran his brown fingers through his thick hair. He shifted uneasily on his chair. He said: "First, I must pledge you to secrecy. This is an international matter. It concerns our allies and our enemy."

"Since Germany is defeated," said Mercado, "we have but one enemy left. I assume that you refer to Japan."

Sanchez nodded. "Some months ago," he said, "my cousin, Juan, lived in a certain country in Central America. There he had many friends in diplomatic circles. This country, along with us and most of Latin-America, declared war upon Japan. Naturally the Japanese consul there was interned. Since no ships were available he is still interned there."

Mercado was making a few desultory notes on a scratch pad before him. Sanchez continued.

"My cousin was fairly well acquainted with this consul who, prior to his diplomatic post, had been an officer in the Japanese Navy. Moreover, this Japanese was quite an intelligent man. He knew his country could not possibly win the war and he desired to make certain that, after the defeat of his homeland, he and his family would be comfortably situated."

MERCADO STILL scratched idly with his pencil. I lighted a cigarette and reflected that international intrigue in Central America seemed a far cry from the corpse of an undistinguished Mexican citizen in the Santa Cruz hospital.

Sanchez drew a deep breath and continued.

"Now this Japanese consul knew a great deal about the present installations at Singapore which, naturally enough, will one day be retaken by the British. So he began negotiations with the English through divers secret channels. In return for the information he was prepared to give them he wanted a guarantee that his family would be permitted to leave Japan after the invasion and that he would receive enough cash to keep them comfortably in whatever country would offer him sanctuary."

"This is all very interesting," I said. "But what has it to do with your cousin?"

"I am coming to that. In this country there was no British agent of any importance. None, anyway, whom the consul could trust. So he called on my cousin. Neither of them dared put these facts on paper. After three weeks of constant talking, my cousin memorized the code which he was to repeat to the British agent when he met him here in Mexico."

Mercado said nothing. However, it all appeared plain enough to me now.

"Thus," I said, "some enemy agent learned of this and killed your cousin so he couldn't deliver the message. Is that it?"

Sanchez nodded. "That is why I was afraid another attempt might be made on his life. That is why I wanted him watched at the hospital."

It was all logical enough to me. I observed, however, that Mariano Mercado wore an expression of skepticism.

"So," he said, "and what is it you want me to do?"

"Why, find his cousin's killer," I said. "That's obvious."

"I doubt it," said Mercado quietly. "Now, Señor Sanchez, what is it you desire of me?"

"Well," said Sanchez, "if you find the man who killed my cousin, that is fine. It would be a good thing. But it will be most difficult to do. There is doubtless a strong organization behind him. I am principally concerned with your protecting me."

"You?" I said. "What on earth have you to do with it?"

"Well, my cousin and I bear the same name. We lived together in the same house. We were quite intimate. It is possible that the murderer, having silenced Juan, may believe that he confided in me—that I, too, have memorized the code. Perhaps, there will be an attempt on my life as well."

Mariano Mercado nodded.

"Thus," said Sanchez, "I want you to watch over me. I am afraid someone may attack me."

"For how long?" asked Mercado. "How long do you expect this fear to last? There are only two of us. I cannot devote the rest of my life to working twelve hours a day."

Sanchez look worried. "I will pay you well. Moreover, it won't be for long. Two weeks at the most. Just until the whole matter has blown over. Say, twenty-five hundred pesos a week."

"*Bueno,*" said Mercado, "we shall try it for a week anyway. Leave me your address. Then go to your home. Within a half hour, Señor Latham, here, will arrive and take up the initial vigil."

Sanchez handed me a card and left the room. I rubbed my hands and said: "This isn't bad. Twenty-five hundred pesos a week and no strenuous labor. What do you think of his story?"

"I think the story is probably true," said Mercado. "Yet, I am certain that Sanchez is an unconscionable liar."

"That doesn't make sense."

"It makes a great deal of sense, amigo, and that is why I am taking this case. Surely, you do not think that Mariano Mercado would endanger his health by keeping a twelve-hour daily vigil merely for money. There is more to this matter than meets the eyes. I have resolved to find out what it is."

"I don't get it. Sanchez' story was a little odd, but odd things happen these days. Why do you doubt him?"

"Let me ask you a single question. When he asked us to guard his cousin he said it would only be for two weeks. Now that he asks us to watch over him he sets the same time limit. Why? Does he expect Japan to fall in a fortnight? Does he expect them to tire of murder and treachery in that period of time?"

I thought this over and came up with no answer at all. Nevertheless, I didn't see any point in examining the teeth of a twenty-five hundred peso gift horse, either.

CHAPTER THREE
INTRIGUE AT CASA BLANCA

HALF AN hour later I left Mercado's and repaired to the Sanchez home. It was a modest stucco building out in the Chapultepec section. The two-story structure was surrounded by an iron fence and a bright green garden.

I went inside and greeted Sanchez who was relieved at my arrival. Then, acting in accordance with Mercado's instructions, I took up my position on the front porch, a vantage point from which I could see anyone who tried to enter the grounds. Sanchez announced that he was shaken and was going up to bed.

Mercado and I worked on schedule for the better part of three days. I sat it out on Sanchez' porch from midnight until noon, then Mercado relieved me and did the noon to midnight shift. Naturally, he had the better of it.

For during his vigil, I assumed that Sanchez often wanted to go downtown or to a restaurant or bar. Mercado would, of course, accompany him. My shift was straight boredom. I never even saw Sanchez. He was in bed each night when I relieved Mercado and he apparently was a very late riser. He never put in an appearance before noon, when I went off duty.

However, I wasn't complaining. It was easy work for the money I was drawing and I could hardly believe that Sanchez was in any actual danger. The killer, having disposed of his cousin, doubtless had solved his problem.

It was during the third night of my watch that I discovered I was wrong.

I had relieved Mercado a few minutes past midnight. Despite the fact that the temperature of a Mexican evening is a steady seventy, Mercado was wrapped up like an Arctic explorer. He wore gloves, a heavy coat and his scrawny throat was swathed in a thick woolen muffler.

He yawned and bade me good night. I sat down comfortably in the big wicker chair on the porch directly in front of the door. There were no lights on in the house and I assumed that Sanchez, as usual, had already retired.

The first two hours passed uneventfully. I had had a hard day out at the Hippodromo racetrack and I dozed off in the chair. I was awakened by a noisy voice out at the gate. I opened my eyes and stood up.

In the faint light of the new moon I saw a poorly dressed peon standing on the deserted sidewalk waving a bottle of *pulque* in his hand.

"Hey," he shouted in thick Spanish, "come and have a drink with me, *amigo*. Then let me in. I have nowhere to sleep tonight."

I waved him away. *"Váyase borracho!"*

He regarded the gate hesitantly for a moment. Then he said: "If you will not come to me then I must come to you."

He thrust the bottle in his hip pocket, seized the iron of the gate in uncertain hands and began a wavering climb. I swore beneath my breath and stepped off the porch. I ran down the gravel path and loosened his fingers.

"Go away," I told him. "Quickly. Or I shall telephone *la policía*."

He looked at me reproachfully. "Ah, no you must not do that. If you will not let me in, then stay here a while and talk to me. I am a most lonely *hombre*."

I certainly was in no mood for drunken dialogue. I told him again and sharply to go away. Still he demurred. Then, as he mumbled incoherently, I happened to see dark motion out of the corner of my eye. I turned my head to the left in time to observe a black figure jump from the top of the wall into the garden recover its balance and dash into the house.

I swore again and turned to follow but the drunken peon grabbed at my sleeve. "Don't leave me," he whined.

I faced him again, quite certain now that he was no more inebriated than I was. I struggled to get free but he held my coat in a tight grip. I put my body hard against the iron bars and drew back my right hand. I drove it through the bars and it landed flush on the side of his jaw.

He fell to the sidewalk with a glassy crash as the *pulque* bottle shattered, splashing the evil-smelling white fluid on his face and mine. I turned around and dashed for the house pulling an automatic out of my hip pocket as I did so.

I slid across the polished wood of the hall floor and bounded up the stairs three steps at a time. I raced down the corridor and jerked open the door of Sanchez' bedroom. I flicked on the light switch and stood in the doorway, my gun held firmly out before me.

The room was empty.

The bedclothes had been pulled back and lay half on the mattress, half on the floor. The window was wide open. I went over to it and peered out. Some three feet below it was the roof of another house. It was obvious that the intruder had left that way, but how had he managed to take Sanchez with him? I had heard no outcry and it would have been a Herculean task to have knocked Sanchez cold, carried him out the window and down from the roof of the other house in such a short time.

At that moment I heard the whirring of a car's starter. A big limousine moved down the side street and went roaring to the corner where it turned in toward the city. Doubtless it contained the intruder and quite likely the Señor Pedro Sanchez as well.

I WENT back down the stairs reflecting up on the awful names that Mariano Mercado was going to call me. In the living room I went over to the stand which held the telephone. I was just about to pick it up when it rang.

I said: "Hello."

A voice, obviously English or American, said in Spanish: *"Está allí el Señor Sanchez?"*

"Está en la calle," I answered. "Is there any message?"

"Sí. A most important message. Will you make certain to repeat it accurately?"

I said that I would.

"Then tell him tomorrow night at the Casa Blanca, three kilometers north of La Caja—that's on the road between Morelia and Patzcuaro. Please repeat that."

I repeated it, reflecting that whoever was giving me the message certainly wasn't guilty of kidnaping Sanchez. After that I asked the speaker's name. Curtly, he refused to divulge it and hung up.

I followed suit, then reluctantly picked up the receiver again and dialed Mercado's number. A moment later he answered sleepily.

"Listen, this is Latham. Sanchez has just been kidnaped."

To my utter surprise, he chuckled.

"There's nothing to laugh at," I told him sharply. "A confederate diverted my attention while another guy jumped the fence, grabbed Sanchez and apparently took him out the bedroom window into a limousine which just drove off. There was no chance in the world of chasing it."

"Well," replied Mercado quite cheerfully, "in that event, you'd better come over to my place. It is rather silly for you to remain there guarding an empty bedroom.

He hung up, leaving me somewhat bewildered. I had expected a salvo of insulting Spanish reflecting on my puerile abilities as a private detective.

I WALKED out of the house, through the garden, opened the gate and went out locking it behind me. I walked six blocks before I found a cruising cab. I climbed in it and went over to the *Calle de Madellin.*

I strode into Mercado's office prepared for a verbal blast. Instead of that I received a stunning surprise. Seated on either side of Mercado's desk were two men enjoying two cups of *café negro*. One of them, quite properly, was Mercado—the other, inexplicably, was Pedro Sanchez.

I stood for a full thirty seconds staring at them. I crossed the room and sank into one of Mercado's uncomfortable and thoroughly antiseptic wooden chairs.

I said: "Don't tell me that it was you, Mercado, who just snatched Sanchez?"

Mercado shook his head gravely and lifted the coffee cup.

"Oh, no," he said. "Señor Sanchez has been here all the time."

"All the time?"

"But certainly. I decided he was much safer here. If anyone had designs on him they would not look here. Moreover, it made things simpler for me. I had no desire to sit on that porch for twelve hours a day."

I blinked at the enormity of it.

"You mean I've been guarding an empty house every night?"

"Every night," agreed Mariano Mercado with equanimity.

I felt my face become red with anger. "What have you been doing? Just playing me for a sucker? I'm damned if I think it's funny!"

Mercado waved an admonishing forefinger at me. "Don't forget," he said, "that you considered the whole deal a bargain. You thought it was an easy job for the money you were getting. Moreover, it confused the enemy. As long as he saw you standing watch at night, he assumed that

Sanchez was in the house. Suppose he actually had been—it is quite likely that he would be dead by now."

Sanchez put down his cup and shuddered. Reluctantly, I was forced to admit that Mercado was right. Even at guarding nothing I had been remiss.

Sanchez said: "God, I wish this were over! But I'm sure it will be only a few more days. Then things will blow over."

"That reminds me," I said. "I have a message for you. The phone rang immediately after our visitor had left." I gave Sanchez the message I had received a few minutes before.

As I was speaking Mercado's bright little eyes were upon me. There was a faint smile on his lips and his pupils were glittering. However, he said nothing when I had finished, he merely transferred his gaze from me to Sanchez and waited.

Sanchez, at the moment, presented a peculiar figure. In one respect I could have sworn that he looked relieved. Yet there was an expression of anxiety in his eyes which belied the look on his face.

He shifted uneasily on his chair. He said, more to himself, than to us: "La Caja. That's approximately three hundred and seventy kilometers from here. It'll take all day to get there. And it's a tiny place. There'll be no local police. There'll be—"

He broke off and stared thoughtfully at Mercado's bare and completely germless walls.

"*Señor,*" he said abruptly, "there is one more thing I ask of you. Accompany me to La Caja. After that I shall bother you no more. Naturally, I shall give you a bonus for this."

Mercado nodded. "I have been waiting for you to ask me that ever since I heard the message Latham delivered to you. Go home and pack your bag." He saw Sanchez start. "There is nothing to fear now. Your enemy is certain that you have moved from the house. Go on. Then get back here at dawn and we shall start."

Sanchez stood up. He walked out the door and closed it behind him. I ran my fingers through my hair and said: "What's going on, if I may be permitted to ask? This doesn't seem to have any connection with the death of Juan Sanchez at the Santa Cruz hospital."

"It is connected very definitely."

"You mean that Juan confided in Pedro? That he, too, has learned the code by heart?"

Mercado shook his head. "Juan never confided in his cousin. Primarily because he had nothing to confide."

"You mean that whole story was a lie?"

"No, *amigo*. Save in one respect it was true."

I sighed. No mountain road in Yucatan was as circuitous as Mariano Mercado when he was explaining a mystery. "Go on. Tell it in your own roundabout way."

"The lie, my friend, was when Pedro told us that Juan had been entrusted with the code. It was Pedro himself who received the information from the Japanese consul."

"That's ridiculous. Why, then, was Juan murdered? "

"It was an error. Remember each cousin bears the same name. Each lived in the same house. It was simple enough for the assassin to become confused. He took a pot-shot at Juan and left him for dead. Then discovering he still lived and was in the hospital he had his agent kill Juan there. Later he found out his error."

"How?"

"Through Ibanez. You will recall that at first Pedro Sanchez seemed undisturbed by the murder of his cousin. The reason is obvious. He believed that the killer, satisfied he had murdered the man who knew the coded information, could consider his job done. The instant he realized that Ibanez was going to print the story mentioning the fact that Juan not Pedro, was dead, he became extremely anxious for us to protect him. Is it not obvious?"

I thought it over. It seemed reasonable enough. Then Mercado clinched it.

"You will remember, too, that when Pedro first asked us to look after his cousin he specified that it wouldn't be for longer than two weeks. He specified the same length of time when he asked us to watch over him. How could he know how long either he or his cousin would be in danger?"

"I get it," I said. "Simply because he had some idea of when the contact with the British agent was to take place, is that it?"

"*Naturalmente.*"

"Well, when does it take place?"

"Now, of course. Why do you think we are going to La Caja?"

"Check," I said. "It all adds up now. And do you think that our enemy, whoever he may be, will show up along the way?"

"I hope so," said Mercado gravely. "It is the only opportunity I have of bringing Juan's killer to justice."

"You mean that same guy who dashed into Sanchez' bedroom tonight killed Juan?"

"I do not," said Mercado. "But enough of this. I have to pack."

"Pack? How long will we be gone?"

"A day."

"Then why pack?"

"Do you realize that La Caja is near Lake Patzcuaro where mosquitoes breed and in the area of the volcano of Paracutin which sheds dust all over the countryside? I shall need several things."

He stood up and regarded the bottles on his desk. Carefully, he selected a half dozen. This, I knew, was merely a start. When he went to work on the vast array in his huge bathroom closet, he would be certain to choose at least a score more.

WE PICKED up Sanchez, ate a quick breakfast at Sanborn's and set off in a hired car a little after dawn. I drove.

There was a pile of baggage in the rear. One small suitcase belonged to Sanchez. It contained, he had told me, a tooth brush, a clean shirt and a pair of socks. The rest of the luggage belonged to Mercado. He had brought along woolen clothing in case of a sudden change in temperature, light clothing, in case the sun became tropical. He had brought citronella and a dozen variations of that lotion to defend himself against mosquitoes, cathartics, aspirin, and a host of other medications to cope with any emergency except possibly leprosy.

The luggage compartment in the rear was heavy with two five-gallon jugs of the triple-distilled mountain spring water with which he gargled and quenched his thirst.

It was late afternoon when we arrived at Morelia, a thriving city named for Morelos who fought and died for Mexico's freedom from Spain. There Mercado bade us stop for provisions.

"Provisions?" I said. "How long are we going to stay in La Caja? Surely we can get coffee there. And *frijoles* and *tortillas*. We can eat here in Morelia on the way back."

"*Dios!*" said Mercado. "Do you think I would eat the native produce of such a place as La Caja? *Hombre,* those natives never heard of bacteria. They are alive with it. I shall tremble in their presence. To eat their food is to poison oneself."

I shrugged my shoulders and stopped at a store. Mercado went inside. A moment later a sweating peon loaded the car with enough canned goods to feed a platoon, a case of beer and half a dozen bottles of *habanero.*

Now, in addition to being prepared for any onslaught of disease, we were also ready for a famine. We all drank a bottle of beer and set off again.

If you recall the shanty Hoovervilles of the Thirties and in your mind's eye add a hundred tons of dirt, you'll have a vague idea of La Caja. Some of its inhabitants dwelt in home-made tents, some underneath old box cars, others in ramshackle huts made out of old boxes and tin cans.

The streets were unpaved and filled with slops and filth. The stench was redolent of decay. Greasy cooking smells emerged from the home-made chimneys. I was glad when we went through it and again reached the open country. For once I was prepared to agree with Mariano Mercado. It surely would have been impossible to have eaten in La Caja.

The Casa Blanca lay deep in a dried-up valley some two miles out of town. Once it had been the ranch house of a vast hacienda. Now, since the land had been broken up and distributed to the peons, it was undergoing slow disintegration.

I drove the car up a macadam driveway that had tufts of grass growing all over it, and came to a halt.

Sanchez looked at us nervously. "Perhaps," he said, "you had better wait here until I come out."

"Ridiculous," snapped Mercado. "I need rest. I need to sit in the shade. Moreover, I need food and drink. We shall go in with you, Sanchez."

Sanchez still appeared uncertain. Mercado spoke again. "It is unnecessary to keep your secret from us any longer. It never was a secret to me. I know quite well that your cousin was killed in error. The assassin was seeking you. I know, further, that it is you who knows the code, that you are now about to relate to the British agent. Come, then, let us go inside."

He stepped out of the car as Sanchez gaped at him in consternation. I wrestled with the bottles and some of the canned goods and followed.

A moment later, after wandering down a dirty, neglected stone hallway, I entered a vast chamber open to a patio on one side. There, seated at a table, was a tall, bulky man in the uniform of a British naval captain.

He stood up and saluted as we came in. He said: "I am Walters. Herbert Walters of His Majesty's Naval Intelligence. Which one of you is Pedro Sanchez?"

Sanchez admitted his identity, then introduced us.

Walters said: "I didn't expect so many people but since I understand our principal, the consul, has had you memorize his information in the British Navy's confidential code, which he obtained from his own spies, I don't suppose an audience matters."

He sat down again and accepted the bottle of beer I handed him. Despite the heat he seemed cool. Moreover, his clothes looked as if he had just left a first-class tailoring establishment. I decided that the legend of the British officers who invariably dress as if they were on Bond Street even while in the heart of the jungle must have some basis in fact.

Mercado had opened a suitcase and selected a Flit gun with which he was valiantly attacking the flies that came in from the patio. Without interrupting his labors, he offered the captain some refreshment.

The Englishman glanced at his watch. "Thanks," he said, with an Oxford accent that you could cut with a knife, "I don't mind if I do. It's rather hot and sticky and I'm hungry. I've got a couple of hours to kill before I'm due back to meet the plane."

I wondered what plane and where. However, I decided it would be indiscreet to ask.

I said instead: "How did you get out here?"

"Motorbike. It's parked at the back of the house."

I dug out a couple of bottles of *habanero* from the luggage. Sanchez had been investigating a huge cupboard at the far side of the room and had discovered a dozen crystal glasses in various states of dirtiness. He went out of the room to clean them at the well. Mariano Mercado, however, produced a collapsible silver drinking cup from his pocket and wiped it off thoroughly with a silk handkerchief.

Footsteps sounded suddenly in the desolate corridor. An instant later a voice said: "Don't move, any of you."

CHAPTER FOUR

SOLUTION IN *HABANERO*

WE ALL looked toward the doorway. The first thing I saw was a heavy .38, its muzzle pointed straight at us. Behind it was a disheveled figure, of about the same build as Walters. Blood ran down his face from a jagged wound in his scalp.

He was clad only in a singlet and a pair of dirty denim trousers. His face was stained and his hands grimy. There was an unpleasant grin on his face as he spoke—in an accent as Oxonian as Walters'.

"Which one of you is Sanchez?"

Before anyone could answer, Sanchez himself appeared in the doorway to the rear of the stranger. The latter pivoted around expecting an attack from the rear. As he did so Mercado hurtled across the room in a flying tackle. He hit the intruder's knees. The stranger in turn hit Sanchez. The three of them went to the floor.

I dashed over and grabbed the .38. Then the three of them rose slowly to their feet. The stranger glared at Walters.

"You didn't quite pull it off, did you?"

Walters blinked at him.

"I hope, said the stranger to us, "you haven't given this spy and imposter any information yet."

"Sir," said Walters, "are you implying—"

"I'll deal with you later. I—"

Here Mercado broke in. "You, *señor*, came in here with a gun. I think the first explanations should came from you."

The stranger said: "Of course, you're right. But I'm so damned furious with that spy, that impostor—"

Walters glared at him. "Damn you," he began, but Mercado interrupted.

"I take it that both you gentlemen are claiming to be Captain Herbert Walters. Is that correct?"

"I'm Walters," said the captain. "And I can prove it. I have my credentials with me."

"Sure you have!" shouted the other. "Since you stole them from me along with my uniform a short while ago, after leaving me for dead at the side of the road."

"Sanchez," said Mercado abruptly, "do not forget that I am your paid advisor. Therefore, you will tell neither of these men anything until I tell you to do so."

Sanchez looked relieved to have the decision taken out of his hands.

"I have the credentials," said the uniformed man again.

"*I* am Walters," shouted the other. "I am the only man authorized to pay Sanchez."

"I have that authority," said the man in uniform.

Mercado sighed. "Sanchez," he said, "why are you doing this? For cash or reasons of patriotism?"

"Both," said Sanchez.

Mercado nodded. "That I can believe. Then, since one of these men is obviously an impostor, since they both offer you cash, I take it that you wish to deal only with the bona fide agent. Is that right?"

"That is right," said Sanchez.

"Damn it," said the newcomer. "I—"

Mercado silenced him with an upraised hand. "Let us not argue. Sanchez says nothing until I give him the word. I am not giving him the word at this moment. So, we shall eat and drink in a civilized manner as we discuss the merits of the case."

The intruder nodded and sat down. I handed him a glass of *habanero*. Walters, quite red in the face, drained his drink as did Sanchez and myself. Mariano Mercado stood thoughtfully immobile, his glass in one hand, the Flit gun in the other.

At last he slowly emptied his glass and put down the Flit gun. He said: "May we, over another convivial drink, hear both your stories?"

"Yes," said the newcomer grimly. "You certainly shall hear mine. Eventually it will send this traitor to the firing squad." He glared at Walters who met his gaze angrily.

"A few hours ago," said the man with the cut on his scalp, "I was landed secretly by a plane which in a little while will take me out to the Pacific with the information I am to get from Sanchez. I had with me a sum of money to pay Sanchez and was naturally bearing credentials and wearing my uniform.

"Some ten kilometers from here I was stopped on my motorbike by a tree which had been placed across the road. As I was removing it, this chap"—he indicated Walters with a contemptuous thumb—"jumped me, slugged me with the butt of his gun, stripped me, took my credentials, money and uniform. Then, obviously, he came on here and impersonated me. Luckily, I'm a tough chappie. I regained consciousness and made my way here to the rendezvous, luckily in time."

Mercado nodded gravely. "And, of course," he said, "since you have been robbed you have nothing at all which would indicate the truth of your story."

"No, I haven't." He paused for a moment and his eyes lit up. "Wait a minute. He didn't bother to take my undershirt. Here, take a look at this label."

He bent his neck forward and fumbled with the back of his singlet collar. Mercado and I peered at it. There was a label on it which read *Jno. Crowther & Sons, Ltd. Bond Street, London. W.C.*

Mercado nodded gravely and turned to the man in uniform. "And your story, sir?"

"I have no story," said the captain testily. "I was brought here in a plane. I was given a motorbike and sent here to meet Sanchez. I never held up this man. I never saw him before. Here are my credentials."

He laid them on the table. They seemed to be in perfect order but, if the first story we had heard was true, that point was of no significance whatever.

THERE WAS a moment's silence, then Mariano Mercado achieved what appeared to me to be one of the most amazing non sequiturs of his career. He reached for the bottle and filled everyone's glass with *habanero*. Then he stood up and said: *"Señores,* to His Excellency, the President of the Republic of Mexico—Avila Camacho!"

Dumfounded, we all stood up and gravely drank the toast. Then we all sat down again, staring at Mercado. He sighed heavily, said, "I must consider for a moment," and walked out into the patio. Burning with curiosity, I followed him.

I said: "That was a rather odd moment to drink a toast, wasn't it?"

He grinned at me and his eyes twinkled. "I think not," he said. "After all there are three nationalities present this afternoon—Mexican, American and British. In the interests of international amity, I intend to offer more toasts before the day is done."

"You have something up your loud and badly cut sleeve."

I was certain I was right when he failed to register indignation at this slight upon his clothes.

"How do you figure it?" I said. "I'm inclined to believe that our latest caller is the rightful Captain Walters."

He regarded me with interest. "How so?"

"His story sounds legitimate. Moreover, a phony wouldn't dare walk in here cold and accuse the man who is in possession of the uniform, the credentials and everything else of being an imposter."

"Maybe he would," said Mercado. "Perhaps the impostor planned to hold up the real captain and, for some reason, failed. Then his only recourse would be to arrive here and tell the story which our second guest has told."

"Have you made up your mind?"

"Pretty well. But I could be wrong. I will have to wait a short while before I can be quite sure which Walters is which."

"How can you definitely prove it?"

He shook his head mysteriously. He said: "You know I am a very well-read man."

That much I knew. He was, and in two languages. But I didn't see how all the reading in the world could possibly aid him in resolving the problem which was before us now.

Mariano Mercado walked back into the room, with me tagging along at his high heels. The two Walters and Sanchez looked up as he entered. Mercado filled the glasses once again.

"You know," he said, "the simplest solution to this is for us all to go back to Mexico City and face the British ambassador. He should be able to tell us which of you gentlemen is which."

"That is impossible—" began both Walters in unison. Then they stopped and glared at each other.

The man in the uniform said: "I don't know how this fellow knows so much. But a plane from Texas dropped me here on this secret mission. It is a bomber which is scheduled to pick me up at a definite time and fly me to

Guam where I will give my information to the commanding American admiral."

The man with the cut scalp swore. "You know one hell of a lot, my friend. What he says is true. Only it is I who must do these things. Not he."

Mercado shook his head and clucked like an old hen. He lifted his glass, said: "To Harry S. Truman, the President of the United States of America!"

Both Walters stood up along with Sanchez, all eyeing Mercado as if he were slightly mad. We drank Harry Truman's health and sat down again.

Sanchez said: "Señor Mercado, I do not wish to rush you, but this is a serious situation. What are we to do?"

"Eat," said Mercado, "and drink."

"I have a plane to catch soon," snapped the man with the cut scalp.

"I have been thinking of that," said Mercado. "Would the pilot recognize either of you gentlemen?"

The man in uniform shook his head. "He's gone to Morelia to get a train to Mexico City. He will return to the States. A new pilot is relieving him. We've never seen each other before."

Mercado sighed again. He pried open a can of sardines and ate them with relish. Then he filled the glasses and we all snapped to our feet as he toasted Eisenhower.

I looked at my watch. It was getting late and I, in common with everyone else, was getting impatient. What miracle Mercado was waiting for to straighten out this matter of identity was utterly beyond me.

He walked casually past me and whispered in my ear: "Latham, fill up the glasses."

I did so, wondering who in heaven's name we were going to toast now. As soon as I had filled the last glass, Mercado swung around on his narrow heels and seized his metal cup. He lifted it and cried: "To his Majesty, King George the Sixth of England."

He drained his glass before the rest of us had time to get to our feet. I swallowed my *habanero* realizing that I had quite an edge on after all this toasting, then as I put down my glass I observed that the man in uniform had not risen. He had drunk the toast to his king while sitting down. Yet, oddly enough, he had observed the amenities when we had drunk to Truman, Eisenhower and Camacho.

Mariano Mercado brought up a sigh from the soles of his feet.

"Latham," he said, "take out your gun."

Wonderingly, I did so.

"You will keep it trained on that man, there. See that he behaves himself."

He pointed toward the man in the singlet.

"Now," he went on to Sanchez, "you will take Captain Walters—this gentleman in the uniform—out to the patio and tell him what you have to tell him."

Sanchez blinked at him. "Are you certain, *señor*, that he is—"

"I am certain," said Mercado calmly. "Tell him what you have to tell him."

Walters rose and saluted Mercado. Then he followed Sanchez out to the patio.

I kept my gun trained on the prisoner who glared at me. Mercado began packing up his Flit gun and those medicine bottles he had taken from his bags. Out in the patio I heard Sanchez reeling off what to me was a jargon.

Obviously it was the code he had so painstakingly learned in Central America.

Walters sat down, balanced a notebook on his lap and wrote at Sanchez' dictation. Sanchez kept on talking for a good forty minutes.

My prisoner protested once. "Are you going to let that little fool betray his country?" he asked me. "How the devil does he know which of us is Walters?"

"I haven't the faintest idea," I said. "But I'll bet you a thousand pesos he's right. He invariably is."

At last, Walters and Sanchez returned from the patio— Sanchez looking exceedingly pleased with himself and carrying an oilskin package in his hand. I assumed it contained cash.

Walters approached Mercado and saluted. Then he shook his hand. "Sir," he said in English, "I salute a brilliant ally."

Mercado beamed at him.

"There is one more toast I would like you to drink with me before I leave," said Walters.

Mercado, who would drink to almost anything, was already reaching for the glasses. Walters filled two of them. He lifted his glass high and said, with twinkling eyes: "Sir, we drink to King Charles the Third."

They drained their glasses. Then Walters burst into uproarious laughter in which Mercado joined him. He shook hands with all of us and left the room. A few moments later, we heard the explosion of a motorcycle engine and saw Walters chugging off.

Without taking my eyes off my captive, I said to Mercado: "I hope you know what you're doing. If you're wrong you'll be in one hell of a lot of trouble."

"Do not worry," he said happily. "Now let us get everything out to the car."

SANCHEZ SAT next to me on the return trip. Mariano Mercado sat in the rear seat with the man with the scalp wound. He held my gun firmly against the other's ribs for a matter of almost four hundred kilometers.

The sun was well up when we hit the outskirts of the city near Xochimiko. At Mercado's instruction, I drove first to the Sanchez house where we deposited a grateful Pedro Sanchez who pumped Mercado's hand and vowed to send us a substantial check in the next mail.

Our passenger, who had been strangely I quiet during the journey, growled: "What do you guys think you have on me?"

I noted that the Oxford accent was missing now.

Mercado answered: "Murder, at least. Latham, drive over to the Santa Cruz Hospital."

Our prisoner moved uneasily in his seat, and looked for a moment as if he were about to smack Mercado. Mercado smiled at him blandly and said: "Now, listen, you. Since you doubtless do not want to tell me your name, since you apodictically are not Captain Walters, I shall call you José. So, José, remember this. There is no capital punishment in our great country. If the courts convict you, you will live. However, if you try to escape from me, you shall die. So sit quietly, *amigo José.*"

I brought the car to a halt before the hospital. The three of us disembarked and entered the institution. Mercado led the way to the office of Dr. Meana.

I said: "What are you going to do now?"

Mercado replied: "This, Latham, is so moronically simple that I am ashamed to do it. Luckily, I have an exceedingly emotional and none too bright adversary to deal with."

I looked at José. "How can you know that? You hardly know this *hombre*."

"I am not speaking of this *hombre*."

Inside the office, Meana regarded us oddly. We were dirty and disheveled. José, still in his undershirt with blood caked on his skull, looked like a rather badly dressed scarecrow.

"Buenos días," said Mercado. "We have come to apprehend the killer of your patient. I take it that the police have got nowhere."

"Nowhere," said Meana.

"Very well. Now where is that little nurse who was with us at the time the body was discovered?"

"You mean Señorita Gomez?"

Mercado shrugged. "I suppose that is her name."

"She's up in the laboratory, performing a chore for me. Who is this man with you?"

Mercado didn't bother to reply. He said: "Will you lead us to the laboratory?"

Meana got up from his desk and led us through the long white halls of the hospital. As we walked, Mercado gave me my gun.

"Keep its muzzle in José's back," he said. "And as for you, José, listen carefully to me. You will not speak unless I ask you a question. Is that clear? If you do, my friend, Señor Latham will pull the trigger. I mean that, Latham. You will kill him if he speaks."

I said, "All right," wondering what kind of a game we were playing now.

Meana opened the door to the laboratory. It was an odd place. Its walls were lined with cages containing guinea pigs, marmosets and various other animals used for experimental purposes. Its tables were filled with glass bottles and cases which held various flies, mosquitoes and other insects. Señorita Gomez looked up as we came in. She looked at Mercado, then at José. Her cheeks were suddenly drained of blood. She put her hand to her mouth and her big dark eyes were pools of fear.

I stood directly behind José with the gun muzzle pressing against the small of his back where it was invisible to Señorita Gomez.

Mercado said: "You may well be afraid, *muchacha*. After what this man has told us."

She opened her mouth as if to speak, but no words came. "He says," continued Mercado, "that you murdered Juan Sanchez with a scalpel. That he tried to prevent you from doing it. But since you were in the pay of a foreign power, since you were betraying your own country, you would not listen to him. Of course, there is no civilian capital punishment in our country, but this, however, is a military matter, You will doubtless be shot, señorita."

The girl uttered a sudden scream. I could feel José's muscles tense in front of me, saw a movement in his jaw and throat. I pressed the gun muzzle deeper into his back. He subsided.

"It's a lie!" screamed the girl. "He paid me to do it. I know nothing about treason. I don't know what his reasons were. He approached me as I went out for my lunch and offered me a lot of pesos to kill Sanchez. But I know nothing more. He's in it as deeply as I am."

Mercado exhaled a deep breath. "I told you it was moronically simple," he said. "The simplest part of the entire case. Doctor, will you pick up that telephone and call *la policía*. I think our work is done."

He turned to me and added: "You see, somehow José failed to catch Captain Walters. Apparently he watched the wrong road. So he smashed himself on the head, messed himself up to make it appear that he had been attacked. He came in with a gun prepared to kill Sanchez. However, in case that failed, as it did, he was ready to relate his cock and bull story, hoping that we would send him out alone with Sanchez to receive the message. Then he could accomplish the murder he had planned."

I nodded. "And it also must have been José who got past me into Sanchez' house."

"Doubtless." Mercado looked over at José and said: "You may say anything you wish now."

JOSÉ SAID plenty. When he had finished cursing Mercado, he turned his attention to the girl.

"Cabrona!" he screamed. "You fall for the oldest trick in the world. I had said nothing. Now you have charged us both with murder. Fool! Imbecile! Idiot!"

Over to my left, Meana hung up the telephone after completing the call to the police. "How did you manage all this?" he asked Mercado.

"Yes," I said. "Now that you have it all wrapped up and in the bag, there are a few things I would like to know, too. First, what gave you the idea that the girl had killed Juan Sanchez?"

"It was a most tenuous theory," said Mercado. "First the killing was done with a scalpel. That indicated a doctor or a nurse. But most of all was her horror when she first saw the body in our presence."

"What do you mean by that?"

"A nurse sees hundreds of corpses. Doubtless, bloodier and more horrible corpses than that of Juan Sanchez. Certainly she can view another one calmly. Yet she cried out in horror, not once but twice. And she wept. She overplayed her hand to convince us that murder was something so awful that she could barely contemplate it, much less commit one."

"All right," I said. "That's not too bad. But how did you know which was Walters?"

"Ah, that I knew definitely. First, consider the manner in which we met the two men. Naturally, the imposter desired principally to kill Sanchez. With Sanchez dead, British Intelligence could learn nothing. Yet the real Walters met us with friendship, while José here entered with a gun."

"Nevertheless," I said. "If José *had* been the genuine article, isn't it natural that he would have entered with a gun too?"

Mercado nodded. "That's why I used my test. Those toasts."

"Including the one to Charles the Third?"

"That was the really important one."

"For God's sake, explain it."

"Well," said Mercado, "I toasted our president and we all rose and drank the toast. The same thing happened on successive toasts—except the King of England. You will recall that Walters drank that toast sitting down. José, here, stood up with the rest of us."

"So what?"

"So, *amigo*, that demonstrated beyond all doubt that the man who remained sitting was really a British naval officer."

"It seems screwy to me."

"Not at all. There was a day long ago when Charles the Third of England was entertained by the officers of a ship of the line. In the tiny wardroom, he rose to acknowledge a toast being drunk to him and smacked his royal pate on a beam. Thereafter, because of the narrow confines of the ships, he granted every officer in his navy the privilege of drinking the king's health while sitting down. That tradition has grown stronger in the British Navy with the years. It is observed rigidly. However, José, of course, did not know that."

Señorita Gomez was staring at Mercado. She said thoughtfully: "You are afraid of disease. I recall your coming into my ward bundled up for fear of germs, *senor*."

She moved toward the table and snatched up a glass bottle. Within it I could see something buzzing around.

"You will let me out of here," she said to Mercado. "Or else I shall release this mosquito. He is filled with malaria germs."

She advanced upon Mercado whose face was suddenly ashen. He backed away as if she were carrying a machine gun. I realized I could not go to his aid without removing my gun from José's back.

As the girl passed me, I thrust out my foot and tripped her. She fell to the floor as Meana raced to the rescue. Mercado hesitated in the doorway. As the girl fell, she cursed and her fingers unscrewed the top of the bottle.

There was a high buzzing sound as the mosquito was released. Mercado uttered a shriek and ran madly down the hall.

Meana got through the doorway and slapped his hands together, suddenly crushing out the life of the insect. But by that time Mercado was at least eighty meters away.

Meana laughed, returned to the room and seized Señorita Gomez. He held her until the arrival of the police.

An hour later I sat in Mercado's office. Though he had
fortified himself with tequila, he was still a shaken man.

"You're one hell of a guy!" I told him. "Suppose I'd lost
my head as you did. Suppose I'd gone to grapple with the
girl. José could have jumped me from behind and taken
my gun. He would have sent at least one bullet into your
precious body."

"A bullet!" he said contemptuously. "Don't you know
that the heat of the discharge would sterilize the bullet.
It would have been absolutely antiseptic as it entered my
body. But that insect! Carrying death to every pore!" He
paused and tossed three ounces of tequila into his gullet.
"*Dios,*" he said, "I shall have nightmares about it for ten
years."

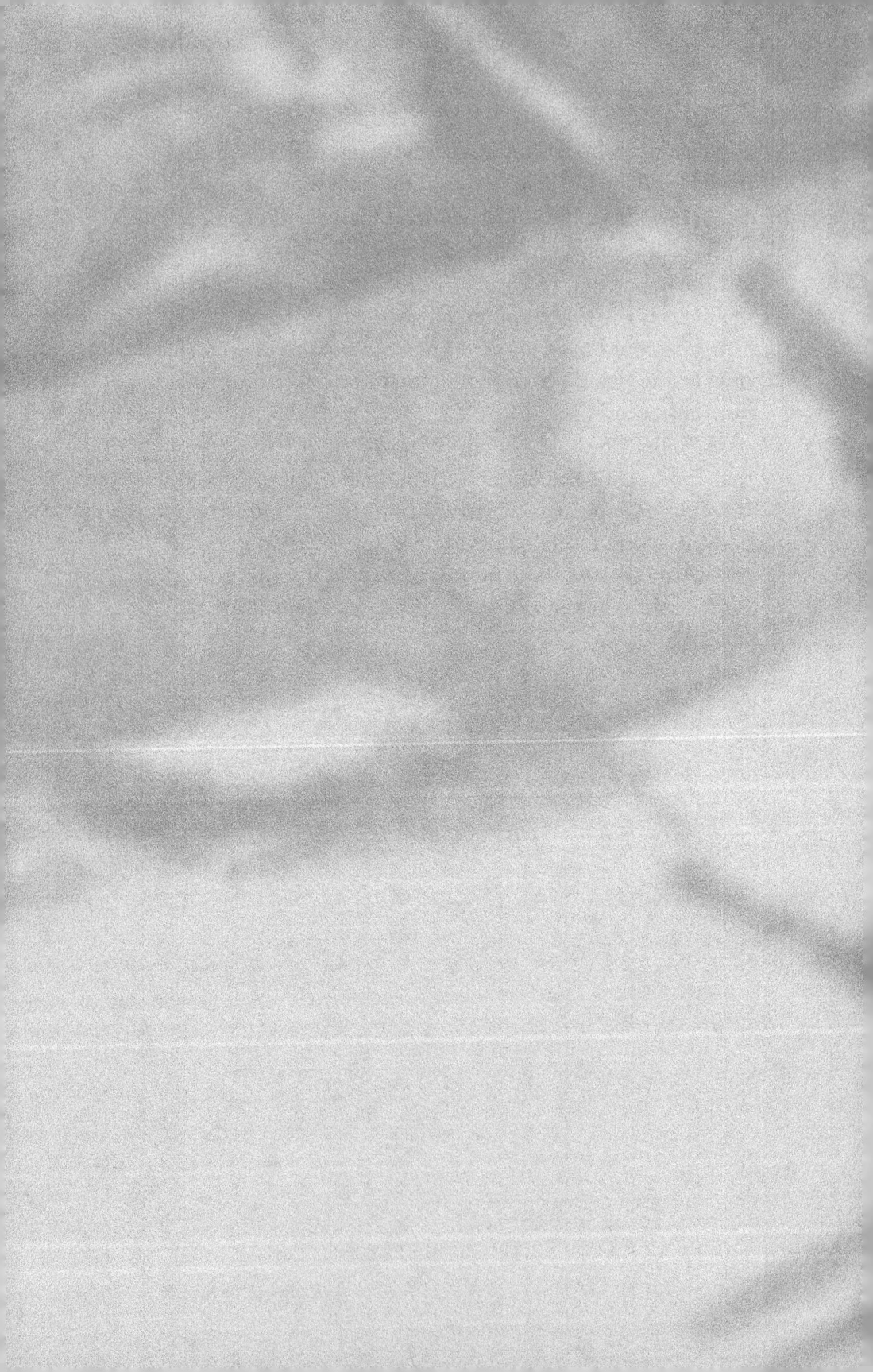

LAUGHTER IN HELL

GRANGE HAD NO
ILLUSIONS ABOUT
AVOIDING THE CHAIR
WHEN HE FILLED LATHAM
WITH LEAD. IT WAS
MURDER PLAIN AND
SIMPLE AND HE WAS
PREPARED TO TAKE THE
RAP. BUT WHAT BURNED
HIM IN HIS FINAL
HOUR—MORE THAN ANY
JUICE THE STATE SHOT
THROUGH HIS FRAME—
WAS THE KNOWLEDGE
THAT HE'D NEVER GET
HIS REVENGE NOW—EVEN
IN HELL.

THERE **WERE** over seven thousand little crosses on the wall of the cell when I made the last one. The dog-eared calendar hanging over my bunk was the twentieth I had owned since that clanging steel door closed on me for the first time. Two decades had gone by—but only in time.

Life, itself, had not moved forward.

It was shortly after dawn when Mullins came to the door of my cell. He thrust a safety razor, blade, soap and a towel through the bars.

"Here," he said. "I guess we can trust you not to cut your throat this morning."

In my estimate of the evolutionary cycle, the best screw in the world rates somewhere below a louse and above an amoeba. I took the things from him without answer, went over to the washbasin and began to lather my face.

I noticed that my hand was shaking as I ran the razor over my jaw. I could feel my heart beating with a quickened rhythm. There was a strange excitement within me, breaking the deadly monotony of all these years.

In two hours I would be out of this crypt of stone and steel. In three, I would be back in the city. In four, I might

well be headed back to this damned cell again—but by
then it wouldn't matter.

IMMEDIATELY AFTER breakfast the sovereign
State of California presented me with the crummiest suit
of clothes I had ever worn. I struggled into a shirt half a
size too small for me and took a good three minutes trying
to remember how to knot the brilliant green tie that came
with it. Then, looking like an aspiring immigrant, I went
into the warden's office.

He was a gray-haired political hack who had been kicked
upstairs into this job when his county delivered a whack-
ing plurality for the present administration. He possessed
a naive and firm belief that a penitentiary could best be
run by the liberal quoting of copybook maxims.

He looked up at me over his desk. There was an official-
looking document and a ten-dollar bill on the blotter
before him.

"Well, Grange," he said. "Now you can start afresh. The
black dead past lies behind. Before you is the future which
shall be whatever you care to make it."

His manner annoyed me but I didn't say anything. He
signed the document with a flourish and pushed it across
the desk to me. Then he handed me the ten-dollar bill
with the air of a Sunday-school superintendent bestowing
a gold star for regular attendance. I wanted very badly to
tell him what to do with the ten dollars, but the fact that
I needed it for an important and specific purpose kept my
mouth shut. I put the bill and my prison discharge in my
pocket and headed for the door—but he wasn't done yet.

"Wait a minute, Grange," he said. "Just what are your
plans?"

"Jim, I tell you—" He
never finished his sentence
for I'd pumped two
bullets into his brain.

I looked him full in the eye. "Listen," I told him. "This
piece of paper you just signed gives me the privilege of
telling you to mind your own damn business."

He blinked at that. Then he shook his head and registered
noble tolerance.

"Now Grange," he said. "There's no sense in your becoming bitter. Far better—"

I blew up at that. "Not bitter?" I yelled at him. "I've just
lived the best years of my life—twenty-five to forty-five—
in a black ugly cell. And for nothing! I didn't kill Henderson any more than you did. Yet you tore seven thousand,

three hundred and five days out of my life for it. Seven thousand, three hundred and five! I even know the answer in minutes. I've been sitting in the middle of a million tons of steel and concrete counting them. Not bitter! What do you expect from me? A spring song?"

"Now then, Grange," he said like a schoolmaster. "Whether you were innocent or guilty, I don't know. But you mustn't let your experiences distort your ideas."

I was a little calmer now. "My ideas aren't as distorted as you might think," I told him. "I came in here with a single thought in my brain, a single emotion in my heart. They're still there, pounding and beating, fighting for release. In another few hours they'll be free."

He frowned. "I don't just know what you mean, Grange. But I'm afraid we're quite likely to see you back here again soon."

"Quite likely," I told him. "My life's nearly done. What matter where I spend it? I'll tell you one thing, though. When I do come back here, I'll go to the death block. The next time I'm accused of a crime you can be damn certain of two things. First, that I committed it. Second, that it was murder. Cold, premeditated, first-degree murder!"

I turned and walked out of the room before he could unload any more gratuitous advice.

THE TEN bucks came in handy. The gun and ammunition cost a little over seven dollars. Bus fare was a dollar more. There was only some silver left when I arrived at the towering Commerce Building in San Francisco. I went up to the fourteenth floor and stood for a moment before a glass door with gold lettering on it—*Roy Latham, Stocks and Bonds.*

The last time I had seen that panel my own name had been on it, too. And in front of Latham's. I took a deep breath and walked in. I announced myself to the girl at the switchboard. She looked up at me and smiled. It had been a long time since a woman had smiled at me, even as impersonally as this.

"Oh, Mr. Grange," she said. "Go right in. Mr. Latham's expecting you."

I blinked at that. I was hardly expecting a cordial reception. I put my hand in my pocket and felt the cold steel of the cheap revolver. I walked across the outer office and opened another door. Latham looked up from his desk. He sprang to his feet, grinned, and crossed the room with an outstretched hand.

"Jim!" he said. "Damn glad to see you. Sit down.... Here. Have a drink. Have a cigar."

He gave me both. I sat down and looked at him. He was fat and well fed. I knew I was gaunt and appeared ten years older than I was. He was wearing a good suit, well cut. I fingered the fabric of my own cotton trousers and felt a chaotic wrath whirl around inside me.

The unaccustomed brandy he had given me burned pleasantly along the membrane of my throat. The cigar was fragrant on my tongue. I watched Latham closely and marveled that he was not afraid.

"Say," he said. "Larsen called me up two days ago."

The name was faintly familiar. I groped back twenty years in the recesses of my memory. "Larsen?"

"You remember. He was Henderson's attorney. He knew you were getting out. He asked us both to drop into his office on the twelfth. That's a week from Wednesday."

Both of us. A week from Wednesday. That was funnier than Latham thought. I kept my eyes on him. Obviously he wasn't kidding. Obviously he wasn't scared. As a matter of fact he wasn't even embarrassed. It was all very puzzling.

He filled my glass again before he spoke.

"Now, listen, Jim," he said. "I've made arrangements with my tailor. He'll give you whatever you want. You'll stay at my apartment until you get settled. We'll start you off right here in the office at a hundred a week. After you get back in the routine, we'll discuss the old partnership."

I put down my glass and stared at him in stark amazement. I was too surprised to be angry.

"Latham," I said, "do you really believe you can square things with a couple of suits, a bed and a job?"

"Why, Jim," he said gently, "I suppose nothing can square what you've been through. I'm doing all I can. After all, it wasn't my fault, you know."

I took a deep breath. "Will you say that again?"

He frowned. "Say what again? You mean that it *was* my fault?"

"That's what I mean," I told him.

He narrowed his eyes and added creases to his frown. "What are you driving at, Jim?"

"Listen," I said. "How's your memory?"

"Good enough. Why?"

"Mine's excellent," I told him. "You see, for twenty years my life's been a blank. Having no new things to remember, I recall the old things all the more clearly. Can you understand that?"

"Yes," he said. "That's reasonable. But what—"

"All right," I said. "I want you to remember with me. Let's go way back."

I STARED at him unblinkingly. He still didn't seem afraid. Either he had more guts than I'd expected or he was a bigger fool.

"Way back," I went on. "Back to the lush days when Grange and Latham were, the crookedest operators on the West Coast You remember that?"

He actually had the nerve to grin. "Sure I remember it, Jim. We were terrific. We—"

"Wait a minute," I said, "I'm doing the remembering." I took a fresh cigar from his desk and lit it. "All right," I went on. "So we made a lot of money. And while we were making it we broke every law in the statute book."

"Right," said Latham and the fool was still grinning. "We were lucky and smart. No one ever put a finger on us."

"Except once," I said.

He coughed apologetically. "Sorry, Jim," he said. "Except once."

"Now let's remember that," I said. "Let's remember Henderson. We broke Henderson. We sent him to the wall and cleared a neat hundred grand on the deal. We raised hell with the penal code while we were doing it but we were nicely covered up. Just as we had Henderson where we wanted him we discovered that a friend of his was about to put up enough money to tide him over, to wreck our plans. So that time we went a step further. We arranged for that friend to be drowned, Latham. Remember?"

Latham glanced nervously at the door. He wasn't grinning now. "For God's sake!" he said. "Don't remember so loud."

"Anyway," I continued, "we cleaned Henderson out. We left him with a couple of grand and an old frame house on the outskirts of town. Then, a week or so later, Henderson came to this office. He stated loudly and in front of witnesses that he could prove we were crooks, and that he'd do it unless we gave him back his dough."

Latham waved a hand at me. "Why go over all this?" he said. "You'll only upset yourself, Jim. You'll only—"

I'd only upset myself! The colossal gall of him!

"Then one day when we were both out of the office, a mysterious telephone call came in. The girl took the message which requested either one or both of us to see Henderson at his house at precisely three o'clock that afternoon. You never came back from lunch that day, Latham. So I kept the appointment."

Latham poured himself a drink and I noted with satisfaction that his hand shook.

"Well," I continued, "I hadn't been there three minutes when the cops came in. They found signs of a struggle. They found my business card in Henderson's hand. They found Henderson lying on the floor with a bullet in his brain. Later, they found that bullet had been fired from the same sort of gun that we kept here in the office. The gun was never found. It wasn't in the drawer where we always kept it."

"Now listen—" began Latham, but I interrupted him.

"I'm almost done," I said. "They built up a sweet case against me. The motive, of course, was to prevent Henderson's exposing us as he had threatened. It was all perfect save one thing that I never got straight at the trial. How did the coppers happen to come to Henderson's house at that moment. Who tipped them off?"

Latham shook his head. He was very serious now. "Jim! You don't believe I did? God, man, how could I possibly have guessed that you'd killed him? How could I—"

That was too much for me. I stood up and banged my fist on the desk.

"What do you mean, *I* killed him?" I roared. "You know damn well I didn't kill him. I was framed. He was dead when I got there. All the evidence was planted."

"Listen, Jim," Latham said. "Now take it easy. If you didn't kill him, who did?"

I was a little calmer now. I'd waited twenty years for this. Another few minutes wouldn't matter. I sat down, took the cheap gun from my pocket and balanced it carefully on my knee. I deliberately made my voice calm and low.

"You did," I said.

He stared at me, then dropped his eyes to the revolver. He was pale and there was a wild desperate glint in his eyes.

"You were scared," I told him. "Scared that Henderson would send us to the can. You killed him with the office gun. You left my card in his hand as if he'd grabbed it in a struggle. You phoned, leaving that message to bring me to Henderson's house. Then you went and fixed yourself up an alibi at the Country Club."

"Listen, Jim," he said and his voice was hoarse. "You're crazy. You're—"

"Sure, I'm crazy," I said. "Try sitting in one spot for twenty years, thinking about one thing. You'll go crazy, too. The one thought that's kept a vestige of sanity in my brain was anticipation of this moment. When that judge sentenced me for second-degree murder, he sentenced you to death, Latham. He didn't know it. You didn't know it. But, by God, I knew it!"

"Listen," said Latham. "I never killed Henderson. You're screwy. Stir-crazy. That's what. I—"

"One of us killed him," I said. "All the evidence pointed that way. And it wasn't I."

I lifted the gun from my knee. I felt a surging lift of my pulse as I aimed the barrel at Latham's head. He put a trembling hand before his face.

"Jim," he said, "don't do it. They'll burn you for it. You can't get away with it."

"I'm not even going to try," I told him. "That's the beauty of it. It's just a plain simple murder. No covering up. No worrying afterwards. I'm going to walk out of here into the arms of the first copper I see."

"No, Jim. No, no! You're all wrong. What's the sense of us both dying?"

"I've got nothing to live for," I said. "I'm an old man. Broke. No friends. I can't start all over again now. I would have cut my throat in my cell a hundred times over but I had this job to do first."

"No, Jim," he said again and there was terror in his voice. "You're not old. You're in your prime. You're only forty-five."

"I'm a hundred and forty-five," I said. "I stopped living twenty years ago. I'm an old, beaten, man. I've been living for one thing. And when you're dead there won't even be that to live for."

"Jim!" he cried and the fear in his voice filled me with a singing happiness. "Jim, I tell you—"

The reason he never finished the sentence was that I had pumped two bullets into his brain.

IT TOOK three weeks to go through the formalities of getting me from the precinct house to the death cell. Then there was another week of waiting before some respected citizen collected a hundred and fifty bucks for throwing the switch on me.

But I didn't mind that. After sitting in a cell for twenty years you learn patience. I wasn't afraid to die. I hadn't been lying when I told Latham that I was already dead.

What difference did it make now?

For five days I ate my meals, smoked occasionally and spoke to no one. Twice I'd refused to see the chaplain. I wasn't looking forward to a life of bliss in Paradise. I looked forward to nothing. Real nothing. Minus even the boredom and monotony that had been my lot for the better part of my life.

I was calm and satisfied. As long as Latham had lived there had been something inside me that was bigger than I. Something I couldn't lick. A sort of driving force, engendered by hatred and bitterness. But that, too, was gone now. I can't say I was happy. But, oddly enough, I was at peace.

I had twelve hours to go when the warden came to my cell. With him was a short, dark guy with a vaguely familiar face.

"Grange," said the warden, "here's someone to see you."

"Listen," I said. "Why don't you enforce the rules? A guy in the death house isn't allowed to have visitors unless they're blood relatives."

"This is important," said the warden. "This is Mr. Larsen."

Larsen? Latham had said something about Larsen. Henderson's attorney. But what the devil did he want with me? I asked him.

"Mr. Grange," he said, regarding me oddly, "there's been an injustice done."

"Well?" I said.

"Shortly before Henderson died he left a letter with me. Further, he left instructions that it was not to be opened for twenty years. I read it for the first time a few weeks ago. I thought it only right that you should read it before—before—"

"All right," I snapped. "Give it to me."

He handed me a sheet of crisp parchment. I held the crabbed writing up to the light, read.

> Dear Larsen:
>
> Grange and Latham have driven me to my death. If their fingers did not press the trigger of the gun that killed me, they are no less my murderers. They ruined me, forced me to the grave. I am helpless to punish them legally, so I have done these things:
>
> First, I have stated in the presence of witnesses that I could prove them thieves. This was not true, but it provided a motive for my murder. I have stolen the thirty-eight which they kept in an office desk. I have attached the weapon to a strong rubber cord. I have attached the cord to a nail in the chimney. After I have pressed the trigger, the band will jerk the gun from my hand, conceal it up in the chimney. I shall be found dead with their business card in my hand. I shall telephone their office, asking them to come to my house at precisely three o'clock. When I see them approaching I shall telephone the police, begging for help. Then I shall blow my brains out. Perhaps they will be clever enough to evade my trap. Perhaps not. In any event Grange and Latham have killed me, and I have done my best to even the score.
>
> Ronald Henderson.

In another hour I shall hear Henderson's triumphant laughter in Hell.

DUMB DICK

CAIN COUNTED ON
SERGEANT SUMMERS'
STUPIDITY WHEN HE
PLANNED HIS PERFECT
CRIME AND THE OLD
COPPER JUSTIFIED
HIS REPUTATION FOR
DUMBNESS RIGHT UP
TO THE HILT. UP TO THE
HILT AND THEN SOME!
THAT WAS THE RUB.
HE WAS A HUNDRED
PERCENT STUPID—PLUS!—
AND THAT'S WHAT CAIN
HADN'T FIGURED WHEN
HIS SCHEME WENT
BLOOEY.

WHEN SERGEANT Summers was transferred from his headquarters desk to Homicide, Eugene Cain got his greatest idea. Of course, circumstance had something to do with it, but it was Cain's brain that saw the opportunity, that juggled three apparently unrelated facts into position of undoubted advantage to himself.

Cain was possessed of a keen intelligence and an amazing store of information. Even the police department conceded that. On the other hand, Cain did not return the compliment. He knew that on a single Sunday afternoon, he could glean more information of underworld activities than the entire racket squad could collect from its stool-pigeons in a month.

Hence, the mentality of the force in general did not impress Cain a great deal. And the mentality of Sergeant Summers in particular did not impress him at all.

AT TEN o'clock of a rainy Saturday night he discussed his plan with Aaronson, the big metropolitan bookmaker. With the air of a man who does not expect to be believed, he remarked: "Ben, they've transferred Summers to Homicide. This district."

Aaronson stared at him incredulously.

"Summers," repeated Cain positively. "Homicide. This district."

For a moment Aaronson was silent. Then he threw back his dark head and roared with laughter.

"Sam Summers," he howled. "That's terrific. What in the name of heaven possessed the commissioner to do that? How will he find his way around? He doesn't even know the town. He's lived in Jersey for years. They retired him to that desk twenty years ago because he was so damn dumb. Even doing nothing he's pulled so many boners he's been the laughing stock of Centre Street. It's a wonder he wasn't fired years ago."

"The working of the departmental mind," said Cain gravely, "is too complicated for a mere civilian to follow. Anyway, it's done."

Aaronson lighted a cigar. "Well," he observed, "the murder business should pick up now."

"It will," Cain said, and there was something in his tone which caused the bookmaker to glance at him sharply.

"Another item of information I've picked up," went on Cain, "is the fact that Georgie Kline leaves for Boston on the midnight train."

"Kline," said Aaronson. "That rat!"

"You don't like him, do you?"

"I don't like any welsher. He owes me ten grand from last year's Futurity."

"Yes," said Cain slowly. "I heard about that. Of course you have scruples about pressing him for the money?"

There was mockery in his voice which brought a flush to the bookmaker's face.

"I don't want a bullet in my guts."

He heard Summers' voice behind
him. "Porter, call an ambulance."

"No," said Cain. "Of course not. Well, I have another
item of information for you."

Aaronson laughed. "You're lousy with information
tonight. First Summers. Then Georgie Kline. Now what?"

Eugene Cain smiled without mirth. "I'm going to kill
a man," he said quietly.

Aaronson regarded him in silence. Murder did not shock
the bookmaker. He had lived too close to the underworld
for that. His shrewd mathematical mind carefully associ-
ated each thing Cain had told him. When he spoke a
suppressed excitement underlay his words.

"I see," he said. "Summers is on Homicide. You're picking
yourself a spot for knocking off Georgie Kline. Well, if

you want an alibi, I'll give it to you. Maybe a little bonus besides."

Cain waved a slim deprecating hand. "You anticipate me," he said. "I'm not going to knock off Georgie Kline. I'm going to plant the job on him."

Aaronson licked his thick lips. His smile held more of gloating than of mirth. "Even better," he said. "Go on."

"Summers is a fool," said Cain. "His stupidity is a surer thing than any race you ever framed. Now here in my pocket I have a piece of paper torn from a timetable."

He laid a finely printed slip of paper on the table before him. He took a gold pencil from his vest pocket.

"Here are printed the departure times of three Boston trains leaving from Grand Central Station. Now I draw a circle around the figure twelve. Midnight. That's the train Georgie Kline is going to take. That's item number one. Here, I have a cigarette case. You will observe I handle it with care. It is Georgie Kline's cigarette case. It has his initials on it, emblazoned in garish diamonds. It also has his fingerprints upon it."

Aaronson stared at him with interest.

"Gene," said the bookmaker, "it's getting better every minute. It's beautiful. You plant the timetable and the cigarette case. Summers finds them near the corpse. He rushes over to Grand Central Terminal and grabs Georgie just as he's about to board the Boston train. It's all very nice."

"That's what I thought," said Cain. "In the meantime, or rather at the same time, I'll be three quarters of a mile away on the other side of town at Pennsylvania Station, taking the midnight train to Philadelphia. You see any holes in it?"

"None," said Aaronson enthusiastically. "Boy, I can just see that rat, Kline, when the coppers get hold of him."

Cain's smile was bleak. "I knew you'd appreciate it," he said gently. "That's why I wanted you to know about it."

Aaronson pushed a bottle across the table. "Have a drink," he said. "A wake for Georgie Kline. I don't suppose you'd care to tell me who it is you're going to knock off?"

Cain covered the bottom of his glass with cognac. He took a deep breath, emptied his glass and set it down. He leaned forward slightly in his chair and said: "You, Aaronson."

Then Aaronson saw the automatic. He heard Cain's voice pouring into his ears as if from a great distance.

"It's Saturday, Aaronson. You won a cold twenty grand at the track today. You haven't banked it yet. Undoubtedly it's in your wallet at this very minute. That's the third fact I've given you tonight. Summers is a fool. Kline is a rat. And you're a sucker. This time the percentage isn't working for you."

AARONSON DIED with less fear than most men. The time between his sentence and execution had given him no time for apprehension. He lay back quietly in his chair, a red hole drilled neatly through his shirt-front.

Cain carefully crumpled the fragment of timetable and dropped it in the waste-basket. The cigarette case he placed on the floor beneath the table. Squeamishly he kept his eyes away from the body as he poured himself another drink.

A professional soldier and a dope fiend can, perhaps, kill a man without a resultant nervous reaction. Eugene Cain was neither of these. He was aware of an empty sensation at the pit of his stomach, of a lifted pulse. But this he had anticipated. His cold will had never been more deliberately set to control his emotions.

He had himself well in hand as he strode boldly through the train gates at Pennsylvania Station.

It was then he saw Summers. A square pillar of ill-fitting serge plainclothes walked up to him.

"For God's sake," said Summers. "So it was you!"

It was unfortunate for Cain that his nervous system did not resemble that of Aaronson. Whereas the bookmaker had been completely stunned in the face of danger, Cain was not. Had he been, he would have stood his ground, bewildered and completely paralyzed.

But he did not. All he realized in that moment was that the utterly impossible had happened. He was like a mathematician who, against all the evidence of science, has come suddenly face to face with a ghost.

His fine mind no longer held complete control of his emotions. Instinct took the reins and shouted orders to his trembling body. He turned like a top and ran.

He felt the bullet hammer into his back before he heard the explosion. The pain as he fell, was not great. He felt suddenly, oddly enervated. He heard Summers' voice behind him.

"Porter, call an ambulance. I'll take him to the station-master's office till it gets here."

Cain's back was numb down to his hips when Summers lifted him. Vaguely he knew he was being carried. Then he found himself propped up in a chair. He seemed to be sitting in a pool of blood. Yet even now the pain was not very bad. There was an odd lassitude in his wrists. He felt as if his strength were flowing from him as an ebb tide recedes from a beach.

He focused his eyes on the big blue figure sitting on the chair opposite. For a moment the sergeant's red face danced crazily before his eyes. Then it steadied slightly, became stationary.

He did not feel like talking at this moment. Yet there was a question he must ask. He summoned all his strength. When he spoke his body vibrated as if he were shouting. Yet he knew that his voice was not raised above a whisper.

"Summers," he said huskily. "How the hell did you do it? How did you figure it was me? How did you know I'd be taking this train?"

"Take it easy, son," said Summers. "Take it easy till the doc gets here."

Cain shook his head. The doctor was not important. The numbness that crawled down his thighs was not important. But the desperate question in his mind must be answered.

"How did you do it, Summers? Where did I slip? God, how could a dumb mug like you find a hole in it?"

SUMMERS SHOOK his massive head. "It was easy, son," he said. "You wasn't so smart. I don't know why they say you're a smart guy, Cain. You left clues a rookie could figure."

Cain blinked slowly. "Go on," he said. "What?"

"Well," said Summers. "First there was that cigarette case. You left it behind you. You was wide open on that, son."

"Wide open? How?"

"Them initials," said Summers. "Once I found that case and saw your initials I knew I had you cold."

"My initials? What the hell are you talking about?"

"G.K.," said Summers. "Gene Kane. I knew you used to hang out with Aaronson. I thought of you right away."

Cain closed his eyes. "You fool," he said. "Oh, you damn dumb dick. You don't spell my name with a K. It's a C. And my first name's Eugene. Gene with a G is only a nickname. You've been wrong all your life, you idiot and now—"

"Easy there," said Summers. "Easy. The doc'll be here in a little while. Don't go yelling like that. You'll make it bleed more."

"Damn the blood," said Cain and his voice was a dispirited breeze. "How the hell did you find me here? What made you come to this station?"

"Why," said Summers, "you made a mistake there, too. I found a hunk of timetable. The midnight train for Boston was marked. I figured you was going to lam out of town. I figured I'd get you at the station."

Something turned slowly over at the pit of Cain's stomach. A sea of utter futility overwhelmed him.

"Summers," he said bitterly, "you're wrong again. You're a damned ignorant fool. The Boston trains leave from Grand Central. Not from Penn Station. The only mistake I made was figuring you less dumb than you actually are."

"I never could keep them stations straight," said Summers apologetically.

He saw the sudden pallor of Cain's face, saw the convulsive movement of his body.

"Easy, son," he said again. "Don't talk no more. You're wounded awful bad."

Cain smiled. The bitterness had gone from him now. At this point there was nothing at all that mattered.

"Summers," he said, "you're a dumb dick and you're wrong again. I'm not wounded. I'm dead."

He was indeed—a full three minutes before the ambulance arrived.

www.ingramcontent.com/pod-product-compliance
Lightning Source LLC
Chambersburg PA
CBHW061520020726
47502CB00006B/2158